HERS FOR THE SEASON

ELENA AITKEN

Reader Note

You might not know…this book (and the entire series) is a little different than my usual contemporary romances.

But sometimes you have to try something a little different, and that was the case for me when it came to writing 'the bears'.

I had so much fun with this series at a time in my life when that's what I needed—fun. So much fun in fact that I needed to revisit Grizzly Ridge with four more sexy stories!!

I hope you have as much fun reading these new stories!

AND…don't forget to join my mailing list where you'll be the first to hear about new stories, sales and promotions and giveaways!
You can join me here —>
https://elenaaitken.com/newsletter/

Chapter One
_____

SNOW BLANKETED the forest in a thick, pristine layer of white that sparkled in the mid-afternoon sun. With the boughs of pine draped over the wooden fences, the oversized bright-red bows tied among them, the massive wreath that welcomed visitors through the front door of the main building, and the lights that would be twinkling as soon as the sun went down, Grizzly Ridge was the perfect place to celebrate Christmas. A place that would welcome you with candy canes, eggnog, and hot apple cider around a crackling Yule log in the hearth. Like a scene directly from a Hallmark holiday special movie of the week, the eco-lodge high in the Montana mountains was the epitome of Christmas magic.

If you were into that kind of thing.

And Liam Jackson was decidedly not into that kind of thing.

He trudged through the almost knee-deep snow, uncaring that he was disrupting the perfect snowy blanket that covered the meadow behind the main lodge that his cousins who ran Grizzly Ridge called the Den. His family had been working so hard to create the perfect holiday atmosphere, that he really should be more appreciative. Especially since they'd invited—no, all but *insisted*—that he join them for the season. Even though he hadn't deserved it.

Not even a little bit.

Liam turned to look back at the house and his thoughts went back to the night before. He'd finally relented to his little sister Natalia's harping about him coming over for the decorating of the Christmas tree. The only real reason Liam had agreed was because he owed Nat. After the way he'd behaved only weeks earlier when their grandfather was dying and he'd almost killed her—accidentally, but still—showing up for a party was the least he could do.

The very least, really.

He'd expected the eggnog, the Christmas carols, and the ridiculously large tree his cousins had chopped down and hauled inside. The holiday cheer he was prepared for. What he had not been prepared for was walking in the front door of the Den and having every cell in his body light up as if he'd been asleep his entire life. And something else coursed through him…something he couldn't even begin to explain.

Liam replayed the moment in his mind, the same way he had at least a hundred times since the night before. The moment he set foot inside the room, all of the noise and activity silenced as he homed in on the only unfamiliar face in the room.

Strawberry-blonde, curvy in all the right places, with eyes so green they reminded him of emeralds. And…*human?*

As a grizzly bear shifter, Liam had an innate sense for other shifters, especially bears. But with this woman, he couldn't scent anything. Except an intoxicating mixture of sweet almonds.

It was the biggest cliche in the world, something straight out of a B movie, but there was no other way to explain it: when their eyes met, time seemed to stand completely still. The entire room fell away and it was just the two of them. He should have moved; he should have gone to her, introduced himself, asked her name, anything. But then, just like that, the moment was gone. She shook her head and turned at something his sister, Natalia, said to her. She gathered up some Christmas stockings—of all things—and left the room. He'd waited for her to come back, but she never did. More than once, Liam had considered going after her, but there was no way. Not really. He was already on shaky ground with his family. He couldn't do anything that might be perceived as… well, it was probably just better if he spent time with his family.

Liam shook his head to clear the memory of the night before, although he already knew from experience that the thoughts of the strawberry-blonde beauty would linger, the way it had all day. He turned back to the direction of the forest and continued his trek across the meadow toward the adventure center, where his oldest cousin Axel, the alpha of Grizzly Ridge, was waiting to speak to him.

"You know, you could have taken the path," Axel said with a shake of his head when Liam walked into the timber-framed building where they stored the equipment like cross-country skis, snowshoes, and mountain bikes for the guests they usually hosted at Grizzly Ridge. With two of their family members due to give birth almost any day and the holiday season upon them, the Jackson family had made the decision to close down to guests for the season, making it much quieter than usual at the ridge.

Liam shrugged and stamped the snow from his boots. "This seemed quicker."

"You know Harper is going to kill you for wrecking her perfect snowy field." Axel laughed. But they both knew it was true. Axel's mate was a half grizzly shifter who'd been raised as a human and had some strong feelings about maintaining traditions like weddings and the holidays. Liam didn't pretend to understand any of it, but Axel was right, and he probably didn't have to be a dick about their differences.

"I'll apologize to her," he said, suddenly regretting his recklessness with something that, no matter how silly, was important to Harper. "I'll offer to hang some more lights or something."

Axel laughed. "I'm sure she can get behind that. There will never be enough lights as far as she's concerned and she was saying something just this morning about stringing some over the gate at the end of the road." Axel reached into the beer fridge that they kept stocked. "Drink?"

"Absolutely." Despite the fact that it was barely after noon, he accepted the drink and had hardly cracked the top off when his cousin got right to the point of why they were there.

"Last night," Axel started. "You said Tonia was back in Jackson Valley."

Liam nodded and wiped his mouth on the sleeve of his jacket. "I thought you knew."

Tonia was Liam's aunt, and the mother of Axel, Luke, and the twins Kade and Kira. As far as Liam—or anyone else—knew, his cousins hadn't seen their mother since she'd taken them to live with their grandfather Gordon in Jackson Valley when they were kids. The story, as far as Liam knew it, was that Gordon hadn't approved of his daughter's choice of mate and cast her out. Years later, when she returned with a dying husband and four children in tow, he'd given her the choice to stay with her children, but her mate wasn't welcome.

He was sick and she wouldn't leave him to die alone, but had instead left her children to be raised in the clan. Despite knowing the story, Liam had never asked any of his cousins how they'd felt about it. No one had. It was just the way things were. But years later, when their grandfather cast Axel, Luke, and Kade out of the clan for failing to bring Kira back from an *unsuitable mate*, it was as if history were repeating itself.

"I didn't know," Axel said. "And I haven't told the others. Not yet. I wanted to…" He turned away for a moment before once more looking at Liam. "I don't know what I want."

Liam didn't know what to say. There was a time not that long ago when they'd been close. When he would have said something supportive or even given Axel a hug. Just because they were all massive men didn't mean they didn't need a good hug now and then. But those days felt like a lifetime ago. So much had happened.

After his cousins had been exiled, they'd gone on to build Grizzly Ridge and all four of them had found and fallen in love with their fated mates, a fact that drove their alpha grandfather crazy. Liam's siblings Ryker and Natalia had managed to stay on good terms with everyone, but Liam had sided strongly with his traditional grandfather. His strong feelings had almost cost him his family.

Almost.

He was determined to fix things between all of them. Besides, he *did* feel differently now. A lot differently. Liam took a deep breath and a step forward. Tentatively, awkwardly, he put a hand on his cousin's shoulder. "I know I don't deserve to say this, or to say anything really after what I've…what we've all been through, but…"

Axel looked at him, waiting for him to finish, to say something that might make up for all the hurt between them. From trying to stop his wedding with Harper, to trying to take over the clan, to almost—accidentally—killing his sister Natalia. He opened his mouth but closed it again and pulled his hand away. "Let me know if there's anything I can do."

It was lame and lacking and they both knew it.

But Axel nodded. "Thanks. I will. In the meantime, though, do you think maybe you can not say anything to the others?"

Liam nodded. "Sure. I won't—"

"I mean, I know it won't be a secret for long," Axel interrupted him. "I'll tell the guys. And Natalia obviously knows. But with Kira's pregnancy being so hard and with her on bed rest, I don't think we should tell her about...well, not right now. I don't think it's safe."

"I agree. I won't say a word."

"Great. Thanks." Axel drained the rest of his beer and tossed the empty can into a recycle bin. He moved to leave, but turned back one last time before he did. "I'm glad you decided to come for Christmas, Liam. Really. We all are."

The comment took him so off guard, Liam couldn't even formulate an appropriate response before Axel turned and disappeared into the crisp winter day. It was long after the wooden door had swung shut again when Liam finally nodded and said, "Me too, cousin. Me too."

IT WAS BARELY two in the afternoon and Bree Brooks was more than ready to close down her shop, Bree's Knees, for the day. Not that it was an option. Not so close to Christmas. Between her online orders and her walk-in customers, her shop was busier than ever. Which was exactly why she couldn't afford to be off her game. But for the life of her, Bree couldn't seem to find her focus. In fact, that had been her problem since the night before at Grizzly Ridge when...

"No!" Bree shook her head and forced herself not to allow her thoughts to stray. *Again.*

She clicked over to her email, and tried to lose herself in questions from customers. So close to Christmas, she wasn't sure how many more orders she could fill and still promise shipment before the holiday, but she was determined to do her best. Her online business had exploded in the last year with the addition of her custom-made pieces. Having a boutique in a small town in Montana wasn't exactly the prime location for a booming business, especially when you catered to the *curvy girl*. But when she started to offer pieces online, it turned out there was a gap in the market for comfortable, but cute and completely original fashions and she'd been busier than ever.

Normally, Bree liked to be busy. It helped the days fly by and she absolutely loved what she did for work. But today she was running on almost no sleep, and when she finally did give in and just got out of bed that morning, her brain just flat out refused to cooperate with her.

She moved to her packing table and started to fill a few of the orders that had just come in. She folded, wrapped tissue paper, and carefully packed each item. But still her mind drifted.

Golden eyes.

Dark hair.

Strong, broad shoulders.

Liam Jackson.

She hadn't even spoken to him. The night before, she'd gone to Grizzly Ridge to deliver her gift of hand-sewn stockings, one for each member of the Jackson family. *Except Liam.* She hadn't expected him. Hell, she'd never even met him.

She hadn't met him the night before, either. Not really.

Besides staring at him like some kind of star-struck schoolgirl, and asking Natalia about him before running away, she'd had no contact with him at all. Maybe that's what was bothering her. The way she'd run away from the ridge and the tree decorating party. Harper would be so upset. She had such high expectations for what Christmas was supposed to look like, especially because it was the first one for her baby girl, Lily.

Bree hated to disappoint Harper. She was like a sister to her. In fact, her relationship with the Jacksons had grown since they'd moved to the ridge a few years earlier. She knew they were grizzly shifters, but it didn't bother her. Not really. They were good people and although she'd managed to keep their friendship at arm's length for a while, in recent months, they'd become even closer. It was fair to say that the Jacksons and all of their mates had become her family.

Bree glanced at her cell phone. *Maybe she should call and apologize to Harper for taking off?* Of course, she couldn't tell her it was because Natalia's brother Liam had made her…what?

Feel something?

No. She couldn't say that.

Before she could make the decision to pick up the phone or not, the bells over the door jingled, announcing a visitor to the store. She pasted on a smile. "Good afternoon." She turned. "Welcome to Bree's Knees."

Her smile grew into a genuine grin when she saw her friends Chloe and Nina holding a tray of coffee cups.

"We brought you one of those eggnog lattes we keep hearing about," Chloe said. "I hope you're not too busy for a quick visit."

"Not at all." It was partly true. It's not as though she were getting much work done anyway. "What a nice treat."

The three women moved to the upholstered chairs Bree had set up at the back of the store in the changing room area. She took the cup that Nina offered from the tray.

"I've been dying to try these," the woman said as she took her first sip. She closed her eyes and made a dramatic show of enjoying the taste.

Bree couldn't help but laugh. "They are pretty good. Thanks again, ladies. This is absolutely the perfect way to get me through the afternoon."

They spent a few minutes chatting about what they were going to be getting their mates for Christmas. "Christmas was never a huge deal for my family," Chloe said. "Except for the presents part." She laughed. "Ask Zoe. We were all about the presents under the tree. But mostly it was a quiet affair, with just our family." Chloe, mated to Luke, the second oldest Jackson brother, was a black bear, whose little sister Zoe had recently joined them at the ridge. She'd fallen in love extremely quickly with Bree's good friend Gabe Wilder, a local police officer and single dad. She was happy for her best friend, for sure, but she couldn't help but miss hanging out with Gabe and his son Ashton as much as she once had. It helped that she liked Zoe so much. She was absolutely the best match for Gabe and the most perfect stepmom for Ashton.

"Well, Christmas was *huge* for my family," Nina jumped in. "But it was more about the party and the food. We had huge family get-togethers where everyone would bring something. Mom would put the music on and we'd dance all night before finally the kids would fall asleep on the couches and they'd have to carry us up to our rooms." Bree laughed. Nina wasn't a shifter of any kind, and besides Harper, who was her best friend, she definitely had the most *human* of traditions. She'd only very recently discovered her fated mate in Ryker Jackson, but despite being new to the whole world of shifters, Nina had adjusted *very* quickly.

"How about you?" Zoe turned the question on Bree. "What was Christmas like for you?"

"Yes, Bree." Chloe leaned forward in her chair. "I don't even know anything about your family."

Bree took a deep sip of her drink, taking longer than necessary to lower the cup again. Chloe didn't know anything about her family, because there wasn't much to know. At least, there wasn't much that Bree felt like sharing. She'd done a good job building a relationship with the Jacksons while sharing only the most basic of details about her own life. And it had worked because Bree was one of the few who knew they were shifters and it didn't matter to her. They seemed to just generally accept that she wasn't much of a sharer.

She should have known it was only a matter of time.

"There's really not much to know." She shrugged. "It was only my grandparents and myself, so the holidays were pretty low-key."

There must have been something in her voice, or maybe Chloe sensed something else that Bree wasn't saying. But whatever it was, her friend looked at her with a tilted head and for a moment, Bree thought she might say something more.

But then she smiled and said, "Well, that's even more reason for you to say yes to what I'm about to ask you!"

Chapter Two

"ARE you sure you need all of this wood split?" Liam eyed the massive pile of logs next to the woodshed. He couldn't help but feel that being asked to split the wood was some sort of punishment for his recent behavior toward the family. Especially after he saw how much of it there was.

Ryker, Liam's older brother, only shrugged and handed him the ax. "You're probably thinking that I gave you this job on purpose." Liam raised an eyebrow and tilted his head, causing his brother to laugh. "Seriously," Ryker said. "I didn't. But it does need to be done and that's all part of staying here. You have to help out."

"I didn't say anything about staying here." Liam shrugged out of his parka so he was only in his flannel shirt. With the amount of work in front of him, he was definitely going to work up a sweat.

"What? You said you'd stay."

Both brothers spun at the sound of their little sister's voice. She was almost as tall as they were, with matching golden eyes the color of a fine whisky. Nat's long black hair was tied back into a high ponytail, and despite the frown she currently aimed in Liam's direction, there was a sparkle in her eyes. She was happy. And Liam knew it had everything to do with her new mate, Cyrus Steele, a Kodiak shifter from Alaska.

Liam may not have approved of her choice of mate at first, but even he couldn't deny how radiant she was and how happy she was with Cyrus. And really, for a Kodiak, Cyrus wasn't *that* bad.

"Liam," Nat said again as she walked toward him. "You promised."

"I didn't promise." He hefted the ax over his shoulder. Maybe if he started chopping she'd drop the issue. "I said I'd come visit."

Ryker gave him a look.

"That's not true at all."

He focused on the log he'd already set on the splitting stump, eyed it up and swung the ax through. The wood split into two satisfying pieces.

"You said you'd come for Christmas." Natalia wasn't giving up. Liam didn't have to look to know that Ryker had a smug look on his face. No doubt he was enjoying their little sister giving him the gears. "And it's not even Christmas yet."

Liam bent and set up another log because apparently his siblings were only interested in standing around and giving him a hard time. "Well, then maybe I should come back." He lifted the ax, high over his shoulders again before bringing it down with a satisfying thud that split the wood. "I didn't say I'd come and stay all month."

"It's not all month!"

Liam felt a flicker of guilt as he bent down to retrieve another piece of wood. He knew exactly what his sister wanted. She wanted him to be part of Grizzly Ridge. She wanted him to make amends for siding with their grandfather for so long. She wanted them to be a happy family again. And for her, for whatever reason, that meant being a part of

Christmas and everything that seemed to mean for Grizzly Ridge. He had to admit, his cousins had accepted him with open arms despite the jerk he'd been in the past. And if he didn't know better, he would think that Natalia's insistence on having him at the ridge for Christmas was more about him forgiving himself than anything else.

Little sisters were definitely a pain in the ass.

"Liam." Her hand gripped his elbow only seconds before he could raise the ax.

Liam turned to look at her.

Ryker stood directly behind her, his arms crossed over his chest, looking every bit the older, more protective brother that he was.

"You're staying. At least until the New Year," she said, as if he had no say in his own life. "You promised me, and you know it. Besides, I think it's a good idea for you to take a little vacation away from Jackson Valley for a bit."

He squeezed his eyes and shook his head. "Away from the fact that you didn't make me one of the clan alphas, you mean?"

It was still a sensitive subject for him. How could it not be? It had barely been three weeks ago when their grandfather had appointed Natalia the new alpha of the Jackson clan. A job he still felt strongly should have been his. Well, maybe he didn't feel *quite* as strongly about it as he had. But still. He couldn't pretend that it hadn't stung when Nat had chosen to rule with a committee instead of alone. The other members? Their mother and their cousin Luke.

It should have been him.

"It's okay for you to take a break from all of that," she said. It wasn't lost on him that she hadn't answered the question directly. "Besides, don't you have a new business to focus on?"

He couldn't help but laugh then because the business his sister was talking about was hers. Well, not for long. He was in the process of buying her out of her internet marketing business because she no longer had time or as much interest now that she was mated to a philanthropic billionaire with more charity organizations on the go than he knew what to do with. "Okay, I get it, I get it." He relented, because the truth was, as sore as he was about the whole alpha of the clan thing, Nat was right: it was good for him to be doing something different. "And I'll stay. At least through the New Year." He bent to pick up a log, eager to get back to chopping. "If it's that important to you."

"It is." Natalia clapped her hands and jumped up and down, which only reminded him of when they were kids. She was always so easy to please. As long as her brothers were around, she was happy.

I guess not much has changed.

But everything *had* changed.

The thought made him sad, but before he could dwell on it, Natalia spoke again.

"Harper will be thrilled."

Something about the way she said it, and the way Ryker laughed, made Liam turn around and stare at his siblings. "What are you two up to?"

"It's not me." Nat held up her hands, and Liam turned to Ryker.

"Don't look at me, brother. Just because my mate is best friends with her doesn't mean that I have any control in this situation."

"What situation?" Liam's eyes narrowed, and his instincts were set to high alert.

"It's just a little festive fun," Nat said. "Harper is running something called the Reindeer Games and it sounds like a lot of fun because we'll be working in teams."

"Teams?" Nothing about what Nat was saying sounded *fun*. "I don't have a team."

"Yes, you do. She'll be here later in time for the kick-off meeting."

"The kick-off meeting?" He shook his head. "Who will be here?"

"Bree," Nat said, as if it were obvious. "Bree Brooks. You met her last night."

His sister was still talking, and then Ryker's voice chimed in, but Liam had stopped listening. His head filled with a low buzzing; his instincts fired off and his bear stirred just barely under the surface at the mention of the beautiful strawberry-blonde he'd laid eyes on last night. He didn't know anything about her, had only just heard her name for the first time, but there was one thing his bear *did* know for sure. She was his.

SHE NEVER SHOULD HAVE LEFT her store. She should have made up some excuse about too many orders to fill before Christmas and how she couldn't possibly take any time off at all, even if it was an evening. She should have lied. She should have done or said just about anything to stop what was about to happen.

But for the life of her, when Nina and Chloe had told her that Harper needed her at Grizzly Ridge to participate in something called *Reindeer Games*, Bree couldn't think of one single thing to say to get out of it.

Her usually sharp mind completely failed her and the only thing she could think to say was, "Of course. I'd love to."

Because what else would she say? The Bree Brooks who the Jackson family knew would never turn down an invitation for something so fun. But that was the whole problem: the Bree Brooks they knew wasn't the whole picture.

And what was worse, as soon as she set foot onto Grizzly Ridge again, they'd know the truth.

Especially because *he* was going to be there.

Which was exactly why she should have said no.

But she hadn't.

Maybe part of her hadn't wanted to say no. Especially after the ladies told her why she was being invited. *To be Liam Jackson's partner in the games.*

There was no maybe about it. There was definitely part of her that didn't want to say no to that.

A *big* part of her.

"What do you think, Bree?"

Bree shook her head in a futile effort to clear it from the fog that had settled over her. A fog that had only grown more intense as they'd driven up the mountain back to the ridge. Chloe had insisted that she join them in her truck with four-wheel drive. The recent snowfall had created some treacherous driving conditions, and when Bree mentioned the way her car had skidded and slipped on the roads the night before, the decision was made.

Normally Bree would be thankful for the ride. She'd never completely gotten used to winter driving in the mountains; besides, she loved the company of the other women. But this wasn't a usual situation.

"Sorry," she admitted. "I wasn't paying attention."

Nina twisted around from the front seat. "I bet you're super stressed out about the holiday season and work, aren't you?" Her face twisted into a sympathetic smile and Bree instantly wanted to hug her. As a human, she didn't have the instincts of the other women, and in so many respects, even though Nina might wish it were different, it was so much easier.

Still, she didn't want to lie to her friends. "I do have a lot on my mind." It wasn't exactly a lie, just not the entire truth. Bree looked to Chloe to see whether she'd sensed anything.

When Bree first started growing close to the Jackson family, she hadn't been sure whether it would work. Whether she could continue to hide her true self from them the way she'd been doing her entire life. There'd been a few times, in fact, when she was positive they knew the truth. That despite the fact that she insisted she was a human who simply knew about their world, the truth was that she was, in fact, a grizzly shifter herself.

At least by blood.

She didn't consider herself a shifter at all. She'd been raised by humans who'd taught her how to repress her true self. They'd taught her how to shut down her instincts, and considering she'd never once shifted when she was an adolescent, she'd never really come into her shifter self. Which meant her instincts were dulled, almost to the point of non-existence. And if she really focused, it was as if she didn't have any at all.

More importantly, she didn't seem to put off the same scent or signal or whatever it was that alerted other shifters to her existence. The Jacksons and her good friend Gabe Wilder had all accepted it for fact that she was a human.

But that had been *before*.

Before Liam Jackson had walked into the den and set every single cell in her body on fire.

Was that instinct? Would he be able to tell she was a grizzly?

That was the worst part. Bree had no idea what any of it meant. She'd never reacted to anyone that way before. She didn't know what to do about it.

That wasn't true.

She was pretty sure that it meant she should stay as far away as possible.

But she couldn't help herself.

"I was just asking if you thought that you might like to stay up at Grizzly Ridge until Christmas?" Chloe asked. "Or if you needed to be in the store? I mean, I know it's so close to the holiday and you probably should be there because…"

"I really should." Bree managed to get the words out, even

though what she really wanted to say was *yes!* "It's really a busy time of year."

"I get that." Chloe nodded. "It was just a thought, what with the Reindeer Games, and all the babies who will be born any day now… But I'm sure we can get you up here in time for all of the events every day."

"Oh yeah," Nina chimed in. "I'm so glad you're going to play, Bree. Harper is so excited and I can't think of anything more fun to get us into the spirit."

Bree nodded along, but she'd once again stopped listening because as they turned up the drive that would take them to the cluster of wooden buildings that made up Grizzly Ridge, the fog in her head had grown thicker, her heart had started beating wildly, and she had the sudden and most intense desire to burst out of her skin.

Chapter Three

AFTER NATALIA and Ryker finally left him alone to get back to the task of splitting wood, Liam somehow managed to focus on his task long enough to get a healthy pile of wood split. He'd just set up another, larger log to cut in half, raised his ax high over his head, and was just about to let it come down with force when his bear growled deep inside him.

"Shit!" Instead of the ax coming down true and strong, it slipped and hit the edge of the log, sending it flying out to the side. The ax landed against the chopping stump with a thunk.

"Oh!"

Liam spun lightning-fast to see the rogue log that he'd just sent shooting out fly straight into *her*. It struck Bree in the arm, and an instant later, Liam was by her side. His reflexes were highly developed, allowing him to move faster than most of his family members, as well as other things. He reached out and caught her as she took two stumbling steps backward.

Her eyes were open and they instantly locked onto his as she fell back into his arms. For a moment, Liam couldn't say anything but then his bear growled deep inside again. He swallowed hard. "Are you okay?"

She nodded, but still he didn't move.

"I'm so sorry. I don't know what happened."

"It's okay."

She blinked hard and looked up at him. There was something in her eyes, something that—

"Will you let me up, please?"

The spell broken, Liam immediately stood straight and brought her back up to her feet but didn't take his hand off the small of her back. "Sorry," he said again. "I really don't know what happened."

That wasn't true at all. He *did* know what happened. *She'd* happened. The moment his bear sensed her, he'd lost control. Liam never lost control. He was the most in control of his bear of any grizzly shifter he'd ever known due to the amount of time he spent in his animal form. His brother had warned about it for years, saying that it could be too much. Or that he might lose touch with his human side, but Ryker had always been jealous of the command he had over his bear.

But Ryker didn't know anything because in that moment, holding Bree in his arms, he was *very* much in touch with his human side.

"Are you okay?" He managed to ask the question again, although his tongue felt as if it were twisted up inside his mouth, his thoughts jumbled even worse. "I mean, really. You might have a—" He stopped short from touching her on the arm where the log had struck her. He pulled his hand back instead, and took a step away from her.

She smiled and her whole face lit up. Her eyes sparkled in the late afternoon sun, and when she spoke, her voice held a trace of laughter. "Really. I'm fine. Please don't worry." She dusted her hands together and extended one to him. "I'm Bree, by the way. Bree Brooks. I don't know if we were ever formally introduced."

"We weren't." He reached for her hand. "Not officially,

anyway. I'm Liam. It's nice to—" His words were completely lost in a flash, the moment their skin touched. His head spun and his bear roared deep within him. He could hear a gentle thumping—her heart beating—and something else…a voice. *Her voice.*

He's a…he knows.

Her voice? Her thoughts? But that wasn't possible. He needed her closer. It wasn't just a feeling; it was a *need.* Instinctively, he moved to wrap his fingers around hers and pull her closer to him. But a second later, she snatched her hand back and shoved it deep into the pocket of her parka.

Her sudden absence left him off-center. He took a step backward in an effort not to fall over and tripped backward over the chopping stump. He stumbled but caught himself. The action was enough to clear his mind and come back to the moment, and when he righted himself, the moment was over.

But what had happened?

They'd connected. Like *mates?*

He shook his head and opened his mouth to ask her whether she felt the same thing, but she interrupted him.

"So I guess we're going to be partners in Harper's festive Reindeer Games." Her voice was falsely bright, and he could see that the smile on her face wasn't as genuine as it had been a moment ago.

She was rattled.

But his thoughts couldn't seem to catch up to his voice and before he could say anything, she continued.

"I don't pretend to fully understand all of your traditions," she said with a wave of her hand. "But I don't see any harm in—"

"Traditions?"

Bree nodded. "Like your grizzly traditions." She looked just over his shoulder, not quite meeting his gaze. "I mean, you know that even though I'm not one, I know all about you guys, right?"

"Not one?" Confused, Liam shook his head again. At the risk of sounding even more stupid than he already felt, he asked, "A bear? You're not one?" She *had* to be. They'd connected. He hadn't imagined it. He hadn't imagined the way he'd reacted. The way his *bear* had reacted.

She laughed, but the humor still didn't reach her eyes, the very eyes that *still* wouldn't look at him. "No." She shook her head. "But that's okay. I love the Jacksons as if they were my own family. And I...well, I guess I'll see you inside for the kick-off."

"Yes, right. The kick-off." He ran a hand through his hair and tugged at the thick, dark locks a little in a futile effort to clear his head. "Okay, I'll..." He let the rest of what he was going to say trail off because she was already gone, leaving him to stare after her and wonder what the hell had just happened.

If she wasn't a bear, then what the hell *was* she? Because she was *something*. He'd bet his life on it.

OH MY GOD. *Oh my God. Oh my God.*

The words repeated through Bree's head until they took over all her thoughts. She all but ran away from Liam and the...whatever it was that had just happened. She'd done her best not to actually run, but the moment she thought she was a safe distance away, she leaned back against the solid log wall of the main building, the Den.

"What the..." She shook her head, unable to verbalize what had just happened. Because maybe if she didn't say it out loud, it didn't actually happen. Because if it *had* actually just happened, that would mean....

"No." She squeezed her eyes shut. "Nothing happened. It's fine. I'm fine. Everything is fine."

"Well, I'm glad to hear it, *mi amiga*." Ella's voice, laced with laughter, had Bree snapping her eyes open.

"Ella! What are you doing out here?"

The other woman's hands went to her massive belly. "I'm pregnant. Not invalid." Immediately the smile fell from her face because the statement hit way too close to home because her mate Kade's twin was currently just that—on bed rest, with a troubled pregnancy of twins. The two of them were both set to give birth any day. The difference was Ella's pregnancy had been much easier than Kira's. "That's not what I—"

"I know," Bree assured her. "But what are you doing out here? Can I help you with anything?"

"No, *mi amiga*." Ella smiled again. "I was just going for a little walk. Trying to get this baby moving. Kade doesn't like it when I go too far away, just in case, so I'm walking around and around the house."

Bree couldn't help but laugh. Bear shifters were notoriously protective. But they loved fiercely and when they had a connection, there was no—*a connection.*

Like the one she'd just experienced. With Liam...

"Bree?" Ella put her hand on Bree's arm. "Are you sure everything is fine? You look..."

"I'm fine."

She really did have to get a grip on herself. Whatever it was that happened between her and Liam, she couldn't let it happen again. It was too risky. It was too...amazing. When he'd touched her, her whole body had lit up in a way it never had before. She'd felt things; she'd experienced a sensation unlike any other. It was—

"Let's get inside." Ella interrupted her thoughts. "I know Harper wants to start on time."

Bree let Ella lead her inside and instantly she was swept up

23

with the holiday atmosphere in the house, the laughter of her friends, and a few minutes later, she'd once again relaxed.

Until Liam walked in.

Her whole body stiffened with the awareness of him in the room. She pretended not to notice that he walked directly over to her. He was still wearing only a blue flannel shirt, the sleeves rolled up to expose strong forearms. He'd been working hard when she'd snuck up on him at the wood pile. Not that she'd meant to. Not at all. But, for some reason, when they'd arrived at the Den, she'd found herself offering to go in search for Liam to let him know about the meeting and then, like a magnet, she'd been drawn directly to him. It was as if...*no*. They were *not* connected. It was impossible.

Her bear was suppressed. All but non-existent as far as she was concerned. There was no way her bear—if it was still even inside her—could possibly have reacted to his. No way.

"Is this seat taken?"

Bree looked up to see Liam standing directly over her, his mouth turned up in a smile so deadly sexy, she wouldn't object if he pressed her back into the couch and kissed her right there in front of everyone.

"No," she managed to say with what she hoped was a normal voice. "Please. Have a seat, partner."

There was more than enough room on the couch to her left that he would have had plenty of room, but Liam instead squeezed onto the right-hand side of the couch. And because there was not enough room for his broad shoulders to sit comfortably, he lifted his arm and casually, as if he'd been doing it his whole life, draped his arm across the back of the couch so his fingertips almost touched her shoulder. It was an incredibly intimate gesture, and surprisingly, one that felt completely natural to Bree.

But as natural as it felt, it had the added effect of sending every nerve ending in her body signals that shot straight through her to her core.

"So, what do you think—"

"About what happened—"

They both spoke at once. Bree blushed and looked away, but Liam wasn't one to be easily deterred—or, apparently, let her go first. "About what happened earlier," he tried again. "I think we should really talk about it."

"About what?"

"Come on, Bree."

She risked looking at him, and at once, wished she hadn't. His gold eyes locked on hers and held her with a magnetism that was almost frightening in its power.

"You know as well as I do that something happened between us back there. I think we're—"

At the front of the room, Harper clapped her hands and shook some bells that were tied together with ribbon. "I'm so glad you're all here," she said. And just like that, the kick-off meeting had started.

Even though Bree had the sinking feeling that spending the next few days participating in her friend's *Reindeer Games* could be very dangerous, given who her partner was, at that moment she was exceedingly grateful for the distraction.

They spent the next few minutes listening to the rules. There would be a variety of festive activities leading up to Christmas, some taking place at Grizzly Ridge, and some events that they had to complete on their own. Bree had to admit it all sounded quite fun, and for a few minutes she forgot that her partner for the games was not only incredibly sexy, but he also had a dramatic and very dangerous effect on her.

When Harper announced that the first activity would take place that Saturday, three days from now, and dismissed the meeting, Bree finally risked a glance over at Liam. He was still looking directly at her, as if he'd never looked away.

"Sounds fun." Bree forced a smile on her face. "But I should probably get going."

"But I heard you got a ride up here," he said. "Let me grab my keys. I'll take you home."

There was so much more suggested in his words than simply driving her home and they both knew it. Never before had Bree felt any kind of heat like this with a man. *Not. Even. Close.*

Hell, she'd barely ever flirted with a man. And the few times she'd actually been intimate with a man had been…well, unmemorable to say the least.

But something about Liam…just the way he looked at her, smiled at her, spoke to her….there was so much implied with a simple glance, that it both terrified her and excited her in equal parts.

But she needed to focus on the terrified part. She *had* to. Because as much as she'd love to see where some simple flirting could go, or what those sinful lips felt like pressed to hers, she couldn't let it go there. There was no way she could let him get any closer than he already was. As it stood, he was too close. She couldn't risk it. *If he found out who she was…*

"Oh, that's not necessary." She deflected his offer. "Chloe already said she'd take me back." She wiggled herself to the edge of the couch. "I guess I'll see you Saturday." Without waiting for him to reply, Bree pushed up from the couch and was about to make her exit when Liam caught her hand in his.

Just the way it had before, the touch of his skin on hers sent heat shooting through her, making it feel as if she were on fire from the inside out. When she turned and saw the way he looked at her with heavily lidded eyes, and that *I'm in so much trouble* mouth flicked up in the slightest of grins, all of that heat raced directly to her core and lit a fire that Bree was terrified wouldn't be extinguished with a simple cold shower.

Chapter Four

LIAM WAS PLAYING with fire and he knew it, but he couldn't help himself. There was something about Bree. Something he *had* to have. It wasn't just a simple want. No, that would be easy to handle. He'd wanted things before. He'd wanted *women* before. But this was different.

He *needed* her.

From the moment he'd touched her by the woodpile, he'd known it. His bear would never be satisfied until he had her. Just once. That's all he needed. Just one night and his bear would be able to settle down again.

But that's all it could be. He knew on a deep level that his bear would only ever be truly satisfied with a grizzly for a mate, and Bree was...well, he still wasn't entirely sure what Bree was. She insisted she wasn't a shifter, yet...there was something about her. Something he couldn't quite put his finger on.

He waited while she walked away, grabbed her jacket, and moved across the room to speak to Chloe. The moment she disappeared into the back room—likely to check in on Kira, who hadn't been able to join them—he leapt up from the couch and made a beeline directly to Chloe.

He put an easy smile on his face. "Bree said you were going to drive her home?"

Chloe nodded. "I told her I would when I kind of kidnapped her this afternoon." She laughed. "She said something about her car sliding on the ice the other day, and I don't think the roads are safe enough right now unless you have a four-wheel drive."

"I agree." It was ridiculous that Bree didn't have a four-wheel drive already. It was completely unsafe. He made a mental note to see about getting her one of the extra trucks they had at Jackson Valley. "But I'll take her back into town for you." He hoped his voice sounded casual and relaxed. "I actually wanted to pop into the Station anyway." It was an easy lie. One he hoped she would believe. "So there's really no point in both of us going."

Chloe thought about it, and for a moment he thought she might say no. But finally, she smiled. "I would actually really appreciate that," she said. "I have some work to do on a new project I'm working on and I could really use some time to get to it."

"Of course."

"Here. Take Luke's truck. I already started it so it's warming up and Bree said she'd be right out after she said hi to Kira."

He took the keys she offered him and with a quick wave, Liam dashed outside to the truck.

Ten minutes later, Bree pulled open the passenger side door and climbed up inside. "Sorry to keep you waiting, Chloe. I just feel so bad for Kira and—you're not Chloe."

"Not last time I checked." He flashed her a smile and despite the fact that he'd surprised her, he was pleased to see her return it. "I had some things I wanted to do in town and Chloe has some work to do, so I offered to drive you down. I hope that's okay?"

She nodded and clasped her hands together. Liam hadn't misread the situation; he knew he hadn't. Bree was obviously attracted to him. He sensed it. No, more than that—he felt it. She was definitely attracted to him. But there was something else, too. She was holding back. As if she feared something. Not him necessarily, but *something*.

"Of course it's okay." Her smile was tight and she scooted closer to the door, as if she needed distance from him. And maybe she did because the moment she'd climbed up into the truck, the heat between their bodies had been undeniable, and he knew he wasn't the only one who'd felt it.

"I won't bite, Bree. Not hard, anyway." He hadn't meant to say it out loud, but the words were out of his mouth before his brain could react to his bear. The last thing he wanted to do was scare her off; quite the opposite, really.

Because human or not, his bear needed her.

"Promises. Promises." Even in the dark of the truck, Liam saw her wink and the smile on her face was enough to make his cock twitch in his jeans.

Damn, she was sexy and she had no fuckin' idea.

"You aren't flirting with me, are you?" he teased as he started driving down the road and out the gate. "Because if you are, I'm going to have to—"

"What?" She turned in the cab, no longer shy or sticking to the far edge of the seat. "You're going to have to what?"

He licked his lips and shook his head just a little. "I'm going to have to concentrate on the road." He laughed because it wasn't a lie. Just her proximity to him, the scent of her, filled him and drove him increasingly crazier. His bear was only barely controlled as it was. "But I like it. I like you, Bree."

She laughed a little, the sound causing his cock to thicken. "You don't even know me."

"Maybe that's true."

"It *is* true. We only just met."

It didn't matter, and he told her as much. "Besides," he added. "What I do know, I *really* like."

"Is that right?"

"It is." Liam skillfully navigated the truck down the icy mountain road and into town. He didn't ask her directions, but continued to drive, turning down the streets using only his instincts. "You're a tricky one, Bree Brooks."

"Tricky?" She was definitely flirting with him, but there was the slightest bit of hesitation in her voice as well. "How is that?"

SHE SHOULD HAVE TURNED around the moment she saw it was Liam in the truck and not Chloe. She knew she should have, but there was a huge difference in knowing what you should do and actually doing it. Especially when every single cell in her body was telling her not to get out of the truck, but in fact to get closer to him. She'd even tried to keep her distance, but that had only lasted a hot minute. It was as if with every word he said to her, he drew her closer to him. Like a magnet that she was completely powerless to defend against.

And even if she could, the longer she spent in Liam's presence, the less she wanted to *defend* against anything. Quite the opposite.

"Why do you think I'm tricky?" Bree couldn't even believe the words that came out of her mouth. She could have changed the topic. She didn't have to lead him into it even deeper. But just as with everything else with Liam, she couldn't stop herself.

Liam pulled up to a small house that Bree recognized belatedly was her own. She looked from the window back to him, the question of how he knew where she lived on her lips. But before she could ask, he spoke again.

"I feel a connection to you, Bree." Now that they were parked, he turned in the driver's seat so he faced her. His massive frame filled the front seat of the truck. His presence was larger than life, but she wasn't afraid. Exactly the opposite. She'd never felt quite so comfortable with a man, while at the same time being scared out of her mind about what that meant. "But if you're not a shifter…"

"I'm not!"

His lips twitched into a smile. "That's what you keep saying." He reached out for her, and when his hand touched her arm, even through her thick winter coat, her body responded immediately. Gently, Liam pulled her closer until there were only inches between them. "And as I'm sure you know, I don't believe in mixed relationships."

That wasn't a secret. Bree had heard all about how *traditional* Liam was, and how he'd held onto the Jackson patriarch's old-school ways despite his cousins and siblings all choosing other types of mates.

"Who said I was looking for a relationship?"

He was so close to her now, Bree could feel every puff of air as he spoke. Her pulse raced, her entire body on fire in a way she had no idea how to extinguish.

"Well then, I think that's about as close to fucking perfect as we can get." He slipped his hand behind her head and pressed his lips against hers. And everything changed.

Their mouths came together as if they'd been created for each other. A low moan escaped her throat and Bree knew in that instant that one taste of him was never going to be enough. Something inside her took over, and there was no more doubt, no more thinking about what she *should* do. The only thing left was what she *wanted* to do. And what she wanted to do was Liam.

Bree shifted so she was pressed up against his hard chest.

Even through their coats, she could feel his solid chest muscles but it still wasn't close enough.

She caught herself only moments before her hands unzipped his jacket. Somehow, she managed to find what little self-control she had left and pulled back. "Would you like to come in?"

Never in her whole entire life had she been so forward. This man did something to her. Opened up a part of her that she didn't even know had existed before. It was scary, exciting, and absolutely thrilling all at the same time.

Liam kept one hand on her, as if he were afraid to release her completely. His free hand went to his lips and he grinned. "More than anything."

Chapter Five

LIAM STILL HAD no idea what it meant that his bear was going crazy with Bree. But he no longer cared. Because the only thing that mattered was having this woman. And soon.

The frigid winter air did nothing to cool him off. With the exception of when he moved around the truck to open her door, he hadn't released her. He needed to touch her, hold her, be connected to her in some way.

They didn't speak as they moved together up the icy walkway, and when Bree fumbled with her key in the lock, she didn't object when Liam gently took it from her and opened the door. As soon as he had her inside, he pressed her up against the wall, only belatedly kicking the door shut behind him.

"Damn, woman." He breathed the words against her neck. "You have no idea what you do to me."

Her hand came between them to press against the front of his jeans. "Oh, I have a pretty good idea."

A growl rumbled low in his throat as he slid his hands up each side of her neck until he held her head still. He took a moment to examine her beauty. Her green eyes, her sexy mouth, already swollen—just a little—from their kissing. Her chest heaved against him, and the delicious scent of her desire for him floated on the air between them.

She was perfect in every way.

He kissed her then. Harder. Leaving no doubt as to exactly where the evening was going to lead them. Keeping his mouth on hers, Liam unzipped her heavy jacket and pulled it down off her shoulders.

"Better." He pulled back to look at her but there were still entirely too many clothes between them. Her blouse was unbuttoned just enough to tease with a tiny taste of cleavage, a detail he'd enjoyed earlier in the night. But it was no longer enough. He needed to see her.

As if she'd read his mind, her hands moved to the buttons. Bree started to slowly push one after another through the holes of the fabric, but Liam had already lost patience.

"Let me." He moved her hands away, replacing them with his own. But he didn't bother with the buttons. With a flick of his wrist, the fabric tore away and buttons scattered across the tile in her entryway.

"Liam!" she objected, but Liam wasn't listening.

All of his attention was focused on her ample breasts, only barely covered in a thin white lace.

Pure. Sexy. Mine.

"Gorgeous." He moved closer and spanned his hands over her rib cage. Using as much restraint as he could muster, he slid his hands up and over her ample mounds. His fingers found her nipples and he rolled them through the lace until they stood hard against the thin material. She moaned and leaned back against the wall, arching her back in a way that pressed her tits out even further. "You are so fucking sexy, Bree."

He moved to kiss her again, but before he did, he freed himself from his own jacket.

"Planning on staying awhile, are you?" She licked her bottom lip before biting it between her teeth.

"Do you want me to leave?" He pressed himself up against her almost bare chest and cupped her ass between both his hands. He squeezed her full cheeks. They fit perfectly in his grip. "Say the word, and I'll leave." He let one hand slip around, down the front of her jeans. Her cotton panties were soaked from her desire for him. The feel of her beneath his fingers was almost enough for him to lose control. Almost. "Do you want me to leave, Bree?"

With her eyes closed, she shook her head against the wall.

"What was that?" He slipped a finger inside her wet heat and her knees buckled but he held her fast. "Did you want me to leave?"

Her mouth opened, but no sound came out. So he hooked his finger up, just a little, where he knew it would hit her most sensitive spot. Just as he'd predicted, her entire body shuddered. "Do you want me to stay then?"

She nodded.

"Say it," he commanded. "Tell me how badly you want me to stay."

"Oh God, Liam. I want you to stay." She lifted her head and opened her eyes to reveal a wildness there he'd never seen before. "I want you more than anything."

AS SOON AS the words were out of her mouth, he was moving. He moved so fast. It wasn't natural; it was almost...

Animal.

He was a shifter. A bear. A *grizzly.* She needed to remember that.

Or did she?

With Liam's hands on her, the only thing she really needed

to remember was to be in the moment. And that's exactly what she was going to do. Bree forced any lingering thoughts about what it might mean to be with him—really *be* with him—and instead focused on the extremely sexy man who was currently doing unspeakable and incredibly hot things to her.

"Now," she said. "I need you right now, Liam."

"Fuck." He groaned. "You don't need to ask me twice." In a flash, his clothes were gone, and her jeans were down around her ankles. She stepped out of them and then he was back, pressing her against the wall. Only now, his hot, incredibly hard, and unbelievably huge dick was pressed against her stomach.

He kissed her as his hands slipped beneath her and lifted her up off her feet. She barely had time to register what was happening and how easily he could lift her before he thrust inside her. She gasped.

She didn't have a lot of experience with men, and he was huge. He filled her completely.

Liam stilled and pulled back enough to look her in the eyes. *Are you okay?* his unspoken question asked.

Bree took a breath and nodded. She was more than okay.

He kissed her again. Slowly this time, as he started moving inside her. His movements were gentle as she grew accustomed to his size, but it didn't take long for her body to demand more.

Bree wrapped her legs around him and pressed her heels into his back, urging him on. It was a message that was received loud and clear and Liam started to increase his pace.

He thrust into her over and over, each time a little harder, her pleasure building deep inside her.

He kept her pinned against the wall with his hips and finally breaking the kiss, he moved his mouth to her breasts. He pulled one peaked nipple into his mouth and sucked, hard. The sensation shot straight to her core.

She didn't know how much longer she could hold on. The

pressure inside her was building almost to the point of no return.

"Liam…I…"

"Come for me, baby." His voice was rough in her ear; his rhythm inside her, unrelenting. "Now," he ordered, and she couldn't hold on any longer. Her orgasm crashed through her in an explosion of color and sound as she cried out.

Bree rode the wave as it peaked and crested over and over until finally she felt Liam take his own release. He groaned and shuddered, but never once released his hold on her.

She wasn't sure how long they stayed that way, up against the wall, recovering from their climaxes, but slowly Bree's thoughts began to clear and the reality of what she'd just done hit her.

She'd slept with a grizzly shifter. Something she said she'd *never* do. Ever. No matter what.

She wiggled a little against Liam, suddenly needing to put distance between them, but he only held her closer. His hands once again slipped down to cup her ass and she realized he was still holding her up against the wall. "Liam…can you…"

"No." He nuzzled into her neck and slowly left a trail of kisses. "I like you here. Like this."

She once again tried to slip away, but this time she was stilled by something else: Liam's voice.

I've got you. It's okay.

Only it wasn't his voice. He hadn't spoken.

Her eyes widened and panic filled her in earnest.

What have I done?

She pressed both hands against his chest and shoved him backward away from her. Liam stumbled, but caught himself. Bree couldn't quite get her legs beneath her in time and she fell to the floor in a painful and absurdly embarrassing slump. But she couldn't be worried about it. She was too freaked out.

"Bree! Are you okay?" Liam crouched next to her, but she was already scrambling to her feet.

"You need to go." She tugged her tattered shirt around her in a vain effort to cover herself with one hand. With the other one, she gathered up his clothes and shoved them at him. "Now. You need to—"

"What the—I don't understand."

"This was a mistake." She couldn't look at him and she really couldn't let there be a moment of silence. No chance for his thoughts to get in her head.

How did they even do *that?*

No. She needed to move quickly and she needed to get him out of there before something worse happened.

"Bree, this doesn't make any—"

"I'm sorry, Liam. It's not you." She turned in a circle in search of her jeans, but the room was too dark. In their haste, they hadn't turned a light on, and the dim light coming from the streetlight outside wasn't enough for her to see what she needed. But there was no way she was going to turn a light on now. That was the last thing she needed. "I just realized I have a really early morning tomorrow and this was...well, it was nice."

"*Nice?*"

He reached for her, but she dodged his touch. She'd been caught up in the attraction and the flirting and the *need* for him that had practically burned a hole in her; before that, she hadn't bothered to think logically what it would mean to be with him.

It was stupid. *She* was stupid.

"Is that all you think it was? *Nice?*"

The word on his lips hurt her heart. It had been so much more than *nice*. It was the hottest sex she'd ever experienced. By far. *And he was...* She shook her head, hard.

"I'm sorry, Liam. It's just...." Tears threatened but she

would *not* cry. She bent and grabbed his jacket from the floor. Somehow he'd managed to tug his jeans on, but he was still naked from the waist up. Just looking at his thick, muscular arms reminded her of the easy way he'd lifted her up against the wall and— "Please go." For the first time, she looked him in the eyes.

Maybe he saw something there, or maybe he just took pity on this woman he'd just slept with who was obviously having some sort of mental breakdown, or maybe he just didn't know what else to say, but this time when she asked him to go, he simply nodded.

"Okay," he said. "I'll go. But, Bree, I—"

"It's okay, Liam." She cut him off. "I'll see you soon. I just really need to…goodnight."

He left a moment later, and as soon as the door shut, Bree turned the deadbolt, slid to the floor, and sobbed because in one amazing moment, she had just ruined *everything*.

Chapter Six

IT WAS SUPPOSED to have gotten her out of his system.

One night. One time. That was it. And then he'd be able to think clearly again. Hell, as soon as he scratched the itch, he'd be able to function properly.

At least, that had been the theory.

But it had already been two days since Liam had been with Bree. And not only had none of the fog cleared, it had only gotten worse. Thoughts of her delicious body pressed up against the wall as he drove into her filled his mind every time he shut his eyes.

Hell, even when he didn't.

The sounds she made, the way she'd thrown back her head and her entire body had trembled around him when she climaxed. All of it. It had consumed him for the last forty-eight hours. But more than that, the way she'd reacted afterward. The fear in her eyes. *Was she scared of him?* Surely not.

But something *had* happened. And he only wished he knew what it had been so he could make sure it never happened again. It had taken every bit of self-restraint he had to stop himself from driving down the mountain to knock on her door to talk to her. To make sure she was okay and…so he could lay eyes on her again.

But that wasn't the only thing he wanted to lay on her. Far from it. And that was the problem.

He drove the shovel into the deep snowbank and hefted out a heavy load that he tossed easily over his shoulder.

Being inside was driving him crazy and it wasn't just the constant stream of Christmas carols that were playing in the Den—however, they hadn't helped—but with all his pent-up energy, Liam needed some kind of outlet for it. Either that or he was going to go crazy. Which was why he'd volunteered to shovel.

But even working up a sweat wasn't helping him think clearly.

He drove the shovel in again before turning to greet Ryker, who'd appeared with a shovel of his own.

"Hey, brother. Needed to get outside, too?"

Ryker laughed. "Is it that obvious?"

"The Christmas vibe is pretty heavy in there." Liam nodded. "Is Nina into all of that the way Harper is?" He felt a spark of guilt low in his gut. A feeling that was becoming all too familiar lately where his family was concerned. Liam had been so preoccupied with Bree, he hadn't given any thought to his brother and his life with a new mate.

Ryker jammed his shovel into the snowbank. "It seems like everyone at the ridge has caught a little bit of the holiday spirit."

"Even you?"

Ryker grinned and looked back over his shoulder at Liam. "It's amazing what the love of a good woman will do to a man."

"You, too, huh?" Liam shook his head and turned back to his work. "Not that I'm surprised."

"It'll happen to you, too, little brother. Just wait for it."

Liam shook his head, but he had no control over his thoughts that went immediately to Bree and the night before. But it wasn't just the sex with her. It was something else. Something deeper. Not that it made any sense at all.

"About that." Liam knew he should just keep his mouth shut, but he couldn't seem to help himself. "With you and Nina…" He hesitated, but only for a minute. "How did you know she was your mate? I mean, she's a…"

"Human?"

Liam shook his head. He still struggled to wrap his head around how his brother—a strong, alpha grizzly—could be mated to a human.

"Don't tell me you still have issues with that?" Ryker turned to challenge him, but there was no need.

"No." Liam shrugged. "I mean, not really. I like Nina, I really do. And you…you're a way better man with her in your life. Thank God she came along, or you'd be—"

"Careful."

Liam laughed. It was still just as easy to get his older brother riled up. "Seriously, though. How did you know? I mean, with another grizzly, I get it. There's instincts and feelings and…but with a human…is it different?"

Ryker raised an eyebrow and leaned on his shovel. "Why are you asking, little brother? Because I feel like this conversation might have more significance than you're letting on."

Liam shook his head. "It's not that. I mean, Bree is just—"

"Bree?"

Shit.

"What about Bree?"

He took a deep breath. There was no point pretending he hadn't said anything. "It's not Bree," he said. "I mean, it *is* Bree. But it's not."

"You're not making any sense."

He knew it.

"She's different," Liam said. "I feel different with her. But she's—"

"Human?"

"No. I mean, yes. I mean—"

Ryker sighed. "I thought we were over this, Liam. I really did. I'm mated to a human—get over it."

"It's not that."

He couldn't think. Liam's mind spun. His question had nothing to do with Ryker and Nina. Not really. It was about more than that. So much more. But how did he tell Ryker that? How could he possibly express what he was thinking?

He couldn't.

Not without admitting to something he wasn't ready to admit. Either to himself or to anyone else. Especially his brother.

Because the truth was, he *was* drawn to her. In an intense, undeniable way.

TWO DAYS after her fateful connection with Liam, Bree finally managed to force herself to leave her house. She had to. Or she'd risk falling further behind and maybe even losing her customers altogether.

She'd left the store closed for one day. It was the first time she could remember not opening during regular business hours. Ever.

But there was no way she could do it. What if one of her friends came in and noticed the change in her? Or worse...*what if Liam came in?*

The idea thrilled her deep inside, but mostly scared her into complete paralysis.

She'd made a terrible choice to shut her brain off and let her body make the decisions the other night. She should never have allowed herself to be with Liam. It was way too risky.

But how could she know what would happen?

Somehow, Bree managed to push all thoughts of Liam and grizzly shifters and her life that was about to come crashing down out of her head and focus on the workday. Luckily, there weren't many actual visitors into the store and she was able to bury herself in filling her online orders and getting ready for the last few days of shipping before Christmas.

By the time the day was finished and she turned the lock in the shop door, she was exhausted from the effort it took to control her feelings and stuff down the reality of what was happening to her. Because it was an effort.

She escaped back inside her house as quickly as she could and collapsed in the hallway, safe from the outside world.

But she wasn't safe.

As soon as she opened her eyes, she was staring directly at the wall where Liam had pushed her back and taken her. *Awoken* her.

Because that's what had happened.

Bree grabbed her head and finally let herself cry the way she'd needed to cry for the last forty-eight hours.

She dragged herself to her bedroom and pulled the shoebox out from under her bed, where she'd kept it since she was a child and had moved to Boulder Creek with her grand-parents many years earlier. The cover was worn and soft, the cardboard corners worn down smooth from years of use. It had been awhile since she'd looked in the box. A long time since she'd needed to.

She lifted the lid and put it aside carefully before reaching inside. There were only a few items in the box. Only a few things that she had left of her old life. Her *real* life.

Bree picked the picture off the top. It was the only one she had of her with both her parents and she remembered the day it was taken as if it had been yesterday.

She was only a few weeks from her fifth birthday and their neighbors, a couple who'd been in their sixties at the time, had invited them for an early celebration.

Mr. and Mrs. Raymond had absolutely adored Bree from the moment she'd been born. With no grandchildren of their own, they'd taken great joy in spoiling her with toys and home-made cookies and would often babysit when her parents had to work.

Her celebration that night had been particularly special because it had just been the five of them, and her parents, who never had much, had given her a stuffed monkey, the one she'd been begging for. It hadn't been much, but in a small child's eyes, it had been everything.

Mrs. Raymond had taken the picture of the three of them, right after she'd opened her present. Her mother wasn't looking at the camera, but was instead staring at Bree, a soft smile on her face. And her father had been looking at his wife, nothing but love in his eyes. And there was Bree, blissfully igno-rant in the way only a child can be of the horror she would witness only a few weeks later as her entire life shattered around her.

Bree pressed a kiss to the picture and tucked it away again. She often thought she should put it in a frame so she could display it properly, and had even come close once or twice to doing just that.

But it was too risky.

Especially now.

Being with Liam had put her at risk.

It was worth it.

The thought came out of nowhere. Bree spun around as if there were someone else there speaking. But of course there was no one. It was her. Her internal thoughts that were speaking to her loud and clear, in a way that had never happened before. Ever. It had been happening since Liam left her house.

No, before.

It had been happening since...well...since the other night when she'd met him.

It was more than a little unsettling.

Bree turned her attention back to the box and pulled out the only other thing it contained. Her mother's ring. A family ring. No one knew she'd taken it. Not even her *grandparents*.

She knew she shouldn't have taken it. But it was the last thing that connected her to her true self. She rolled it between her fingers for a moment before letting it fall into her palm.

She traced one finger along the engraved words etched into the gold band—*Sterling*.

Chapter Seven

SATURDAY MORNING DAWNED BRIGHT, crisp, and cold. The moment Liam woke up, he knew something was wrong. His bedroom was cold. And not just a little it's-a-winter-day-put-on-an-extra-pair-of-socks cold. But more of a the-heater-has-died-you're-going-to-need-to-start-a-fire kind of cold.

His foot hit the hardwood floor and he immediately snatched it back up and tucked it under the quilt again. He'd been staying in one of the guest rooms in the Den, and although the room was cozy, and his bed was definitely a warm place to be, he could think of something—or someone—who would make it a whole lot cozier.

The moment he allowed Bree into his thoughts, his body reacted with force.

No way was he getting out of bed now.

Not when he had memories of his night with Bree to keep him warm. And he was definitely warm.

Liam let his hand drift down between his legs, where he was already hot and hard. *Damn.* If he was this turned on by the memory of what they'd done together, how the hell was he going to react when he saw her again?

He wrapped his hand around his cock and closed his eyes. An image of Bree popped in: pushed up against the wall, her heavy, gorgeous tits heaving against the thin lace of her bra, her nipples hard and pink, standing proud and ready for his attention.

Liam let his imagination fast-forward to the way she'd thrown her head back and the noises that escaped her throat as he'd taken her up against the wall. *Faster. Harder. Until finally she*—

"Liam!"

What the—

"Liam!" His brother yelled his name again, followed by a heavy pounding on his door. "Are you awake?"

He groaned, pulled the blankets up over his head and moved to roll over to finish what he'd started, but it was no use. The moment was gone. Besides, Ryker didn't seem to be letting up anytime soon.

"Liam!" More banging on the door. Followed by a jiggle of the door handle. "Wake up! It's an emergency!"

There was no help for it. With a groan, Liam slipped from the bed and tugged a pair of sweats on over his naked body. He ignored the cold as he padded across the room. His brief moment of memory was enough to heat him through.

"I'm up. I'm—"

The moment he unlatched the lock, the door flew open and a wild-eyed Ryker flew inside the room.

"What the hell, Ryker. I was—"

"I don't give a shit what you were doing." That was probably a good thing, because Liam didn't actually want to explain to his brother what it was he *had* been doing, after all. "The heat's out."

"I noticed." Liam crossed his arms over his chest.

"It's about a million degrees below outside and if we don't get the heat on, the pipes could freeze."

Liam turned to grab a sweater. He was handy with mechanical issues, which was probably why Ryker had come to wake him. But of course, all of his cousins were handy with that kind of thing, too. Especially Kade. He shook his head. That didn't matter. If he could help, he would. "Okay, I'll take a look at it. Let me get—"

"No time!"

Liam snatched a hoodie from the back of the chair where he'd thrown it the night before and turned back to his normally calm and collected brother. "What is going on? It's just a furnace. I'm sure I can get it going in no time."

"It's not just the furnace." His eyes grew wider. "It's Kira. She's in labor or something. I don't know, but everyone is freaking out and…well, I…"

Liam laughed. "And you have no idea what to do." He slapped his brother on the back. "It's a good thing it's not your mate or your baby. You're going to have to toughen up before it's your turn."

Ryker's face turned white and he grabbed the doorframe.

Liam only laughed again. "That might have been the wrong thing to say," he admitted. "Don't worry, Ryker. I'm sure you'll handle things much better when it's your turn."

Liam changed quickly into a pair of jeans and slipped some shoes on. "Come on. Let's go help where we can, okay? Maybe a good place will be to start with the furnace."

Ryker, like so many alpha male grizzlies, was clearly not good at handling a woman in labor. Particularly when that woman was involved in a dangerous pregnancy. It wasn't uncommon to see it. Liam's grandfather had explained it to him years ago. It had something to do with the alpha males always being in control of a situation, and therefore they were able to remain calm in even the most stressful situations. But with labor, they were completely out of control and often struggled with being unable to help out.

Liam had never actually seen Ryker's reaction to a woman in labor before, but when he got down to the main room of the Den, it didn't take long to see that Ryker wasn't the only one affected. Axel had taken charge of the situation; having had experience with his own child, he knew exactly what needed to be done. Which, in this case, was getting Kira down to town and to the hospital as quickly as possible.

The only problem was that the road was covered in snow, and the plow was frozen from the subzero temperatures. A situation that had Luke, who was in charge of the plow, beside himself with concern.

Kade paced the floor, trying not to look toward the room where they'd put his twin sister, where most of the females—including his own very pregnant mate—were currently attending to Kira.

"Where's everyone else?" Liam asked Axel, who stared intently at his phone.

"Nash is with Kira, of course," he looked up and said. "He's actually handling all of this pretty well. Kira's in a lot of pain." He shook his head, concern for his little sister written all over his face. "We need to get her to the hospital fast. I don't even know why we didn't…it's too late for worrying about what we should have done," he corrected himself quickly and refocused. "Gabe is in town, and he's working on getting one of the town's snowplows to clear our road as a special favor, but I—"

They were interrupted by the front door slamming open so hard it hit the opposite wall. "What the—"

"I have a solution." Cyrus Steele, Natalia's mate, filled the doorway. As a Kodiak, he was bigger than even the biggest of the Jackson alphas and richer than all of them combined—a few times over. "We need to get Kira ready to go." He walked inside, over to where Liam and Axel stood.

"How are you going to get her there?" Liam asked.

"The roads are covered from last night's snowfall. It's too risky." Axel shook his head. "We need to put heat in that garage. The plow should have started. It's not—"

"Don't worry about that," Cyrus interrupted him. "I have a helicopter coming. He's going to land in fifteen minutes."

Liam's mouth dropped open. *A helicopter? Of course. Leave it to the billionaire.*

"But I need every able body out there shoveling a pad for him to land."

"In the meadow?"

Liam almost laughed out loud at Axel's expression because no doubt he was thinking about the perfect snow-covered meadow his mate had been admiring only a few days earlier. But before he could say anything, Axel recovered and started yelling out orders for everyone who could to grab a shovel.

BREE WOKE to the sound of her cell phone. Bleary-eyed, she looked first to the clock on the other side of the room.

It was already almost nine.

She'd slept in.

She located the phone and pressed the button to accept the call without looking at it.

"Hello?"

"Bree? You need to get to the hospital."

She shook her head clear. "What?"

"The hospital," the voice that sounded a lot like Chloe's said again. "Can you get there?"

Bree lifted the phone away from her ear long enough to see the name on her phone. It *was* Chloe. "Chloe?"

"Yes. Can you, Bree?"

"Get to the hospital? Of course. Why?" Her head was clearly still clouded from sleep, but she made every effort to get her brain caught up with whatever it was that was going on over the phone. "Is everything okay?"

"No."

Bree's heart stopped.

"I mean, yes." On the other end of the phone, Bree heard Chloe take a breath. "I'm sorry," she said, a little calmer. "It's been a crazy morning around here. We have no heat and the roads are covered in snow and we couldn't get her down to—"

"Get who? Is Kira okay?" Once again, Bree's heart stopped. Being woken up in such a frantic way was not good for a person. "Is it the babies? Is she—"

"She's on her way to the hospital." Chloe cut her off. "In a helicopter with Nash. But none of us can get there because the roads and…can you get there? Can you be there for her and let us all know how things are going?"

"Of course." She answered automatically as she got out of bed and started digging through her dresser for clothes. "I'll get there right away," she said, forgetting how only the night before she'd cried herself to sleep after making the decision to keep her distance from the Jacksons. It was the safest thing for her now that…well, now that everything had changed.

But all of that was forgotten because her friend needed her. "I'll text you as soon as I get there," she said to Chloe before hanging up to finish getting ready.

Nothing mattered. Not her history. Not her new feelings and *instincts* that had started pushing their way through. Nothing mattered except being there for Kira.

Everything else could wait.

But not for long.

LIAM'S WORK wasn't done after they finished shoveling a landing pad for the helicopter. He still had a furnace to fix.

Although, as soon as Kira was safely loaded with Nash by her side, and they'd all watched the chopper lift off from the safety of the porch, and the immediate crisis was behind them, Liam suddenly had a few more helpers for the job. With Luke's help, they'd made short work of sorting out the furnace, and it wasn't long before heat was once again rushing through the walls and warming up the house.

The mouthwatering scent of bacon greeted them when they came up from the basement. It turned out that with Kira gone, and nothing left to do but worry, everyone had found their own ways to occupy their time, and for Kade, Ella, and Harper, that meant cooking up a massive breakfast for everyone.

"After we eat, I can help you take a look at that snowplow," Liam told Luke as they sat down. "I'm sure we'll be able to get it started."

"I appreciate that, man." Luke took a freshly baked biscuit and handed Liam the platter. "I have a feeling there will be more than a few people who will be dying to get down to town to see Kira."

"And the babies!" Chloe called from the other side of the table. "I have a feeling those babies are coming this afternoon."

"I bet they'll already be born by the time we get there." Harper groaned. "I hope she's doing okay. It's not easy." She looked over to baby Lily, who sat, happily smashing scrambled egg on her highchair tray. "Worth it," Harper added. "But not easy."

"She's an alpha grizzly, though, don't forget." Axel put his hand lovingly on his mate's arm. "She probably won't have as hard a time as you did, babe. Besides, you did great."

"Thanks." She smiled. "But her pregnancy…"

"She's got bi-shifter babies." Kade shook his head. He stuck a piece of bacon in his mouth. "Wolves…who knows how that will…it's unprecedented. I don't know of anyone who…"

The table fell quiet because the truth, the way Liam understood it, was that no one knew of anyone else who'd ever successfully given birth to a bi-shifter baby, let alone two of them. Half breeds? Yes. But mixed species? It almost never happened that a bear took a mate that wasn't a bear. In fact, Liam had never heard of it before Kira and Nash. No one had any idea of what would happen.

"She'll be fine," Natalia said with an authority that made everyone listen. "She's strong. And stubborn. And a Jackson. Kira will be absolutely fine and so will those babies. Why don't we talk about something else?" She looked around the table and when no one said anything, Liam spoke up.

"I know things might be put on pause a little bit," he said. "But what's the first event for the Reindeer Games?" He genuinely wanted to know, because participating in Harper's ridiculous activity would mean that he'd be guaranteed to see Bree again. And he couldn't wait to get her alone. Because not only did he want to kiss her again so badly he could almost taste her lips on his, he had more than a few questions for her. And he was determined to get answers.

"I had a cookie decorating contest scheduled for tonight, but now…well, I think I might have to cut back on some of the activities I had planned."

"There's no reason we can't still do that."

Harper tipped her head and stared at Liam.

"I'm serious," he began. "I mean, Kira's in the hospital, I get that." He looked at Natalia, who gave him a look of bewilderment. He wasn't trying to be insensitive, although he was one hundred percent sure that's exactly how it was coming off. "And I know we're all worried about her and want to do everything we can…" He looked around the table.

"Liam, this is—"

"Hear me out." He cut his sister off. "I just think that instead of sitting around worrying about things, we could keep busy." He didn't bother to add that he'd be more than happy to keep busy with Bree. "Besides, I'm sure everything with Kira will go smoothly and she wouldn't want us to stop the games after all the organizing you've already done, Harper."

It was the right thing to say. Harper looked at her plate for a moment before looking up again. "You're right." She looked to Chloe, who nodded in agreement. "She really wouldn't want us all to put off the celebrations."

"Especially since she wasn't able to take part anyway," Chloe agreed.

"But I still want to get down there as soon as possible, so not today." Harper shook her head with finality. "At least not until we know she's okay and have a chance to see her."

Disappointment flooded through Liam but he knew she was right. Besides, Bree was at the hospital with Kira anyway, and he didn't have to ask her to know that she wasn't going to leave her friend's side. Not for a cookie decorating contest. *And not for him.*

The thought hit him in the heart. He may have spent the better part of the last few days trying to figure her out and why exactly she was so hot and cold with him. And even more pressing, what exactly it was that had happened between them the other night. Because it had been more than sex. *A lot more.*

But that didn't make sense. He'd had sex with human women before. It had never been like that.

Not. Even. Close.

His appetite gone, Liam dropped the biscuit he was still holding and pushed up from the table.

"Where are you going?" Natalia stopped him. "We're not done eating."

He turned and for the first time noticed that everyone around the table was silent and watching him.

"Are you okay, Liam?" Ryker sat back in his chair, watching him closely. "You don't look right, brother."

Liam shook his head. "Just thinking about everything that needs to get done," he lied. "I'm going to take a look at that plow, if it's all the same to you guys?" He didn't wait for an answer. "The sooner we get the roads cleared, the sooner you all can get into town and to Kira."

And I can get to Bree.

Chapter Eight

"I CAN'T BELIEVE how amazing you are." Bree shook her head and stared at her friend in awe. "You made that look... wow." She turned from Kira to the plastic bassinets next to the bed that held the two impossibly tiny newborns. "They are absolutely perfect."

Despite being exhausted, Kira's smile was bright as she stared at her babies. "They are, aren't they?"

"You know it." Nash leaned over and gave his mate a kiss on the cheek. "Can I get you anything, babe? Do you need to rest?"

"Not yet." She shook her head slightly, but didn't look away from the twins.

Everything had happened so quickly. Bree had arrived at the hospital just as the helicopter had landed, and had fortunately been allowed to stay with Kira and Nash for the labor and delivery. She'd been right there, holding Kira's hand and encouraging her to push only moments later.

The twins had come into the world quickly and Kira was already in active labor by the time she arrived at the hospital. The doctor, fortunately, was familiar with shifter pregnancies and knew what to expect, but Bree, as a complete and total newbie, now, almost an hour later, was still in shock at how fast it had all happened.

The doctor had been worried about Kira's blood pressure and there had been one touch-and-go moment right before delivering the first baby, where they almost elected to perform a Cesarean section, but Kira had insisted on pushing.

And only moments later, her baby boy was born, with his twin sister following shortly.

"I still can't believe it," Kira said. "For almost nine months they gave me such a hard time and then the actual labor happens and..." She chuckled. "Well, I didn't expect them to go so easy on me."

"Don't worry, babe." Nash grinned. "I'm sure they'll give us plenty of hard times in the years to come."

The new parents tipped their heads together as they admired their new family and Bree felt a clench in her gut. She was intruding. She moved to stand, but Nash stopped her.

"No. Stay." He held his hand out. "I need to run down to the cafeteria and make a few calls and grab some coffee. Besides, the others should be here soon. Get your cuddles in while you can."

Uncertain, Bree looked to Kira, who nodded. "Stay," she said. "Please."

"Of course." She settled back in her chair. "Besides, I don't think I'll ever get enough of looking at those two adorable faces." It was true. She hadn't been able to take her eyes off them from the second they were born. They were both absolutely perfect, with full heads of dark hair and striking blue eyes. Not that they'd opened their eyes much. After some initial fussing and crying, they'd fallen asleep quickly. "I know I keep saying it, Kira. But they're so amazing."

She laughed. "Why don't you hold one?"

Bree shook her head automatically, but at the same time moved to pick up the little boy.

The baby fit in Bree's arms naturally. She cuddled him close to her breast and stared down at his chubby cheeks. The baby, who still hadn't been named, chose that moment to open his eyes, and when he looked up at her, she completely melted.

You'll have your own someday.

The thought came out of nowhere. She'd never thought about having children before. Not really. Not after the way she'd grown up. Her history…could she? Would she even want to?

Of course.

"Bree?"

Kira's voice reached her through the fog that had settled over her and pulled her out of her thoughts. She blinked once and then again until her friend came into focus.

"Are you okay? You kind of drifted away for a minute."

Bree nodded.

"You seem kind of…" Kira screwed up her face and examined her with a critical eye. "You're different. You seem kind of—"

"It must be all the excitement of the day," Bree interrupted her. She took one last look at the infant and handed him to Kira. "It's been kind of crazy, right? I mean…"

"It has," Kira agreed. "But my instincts are usually pretty right-on. Are you—"

"You just gave birth, Kira." Bree forced a laugh. "I don't know much about how the shifter thing works, but your instincts must be a little off-kilter now, right? I mean, look at what you just went through."

She needed to get out of there. With everything happening, she hadn't even worried about the change in her. About what her shifter friends might notice about her now that she'd…*what?*

It's not as if she'd mated.

Not yet.

Damn, that voice needed to shut the hell up.

"I really should go," Bree said. "You're going to have so much company right away and—"

"Knock knock."

Bree spun around and had never been so glad to see her friends.

Harper, Chloe, and Ella all stood at the door to the room, wearing eager smiles. "Can we come in?"

"You made it!"

The ladies clambered into the room and in the excitement of the moment, Bree grabbed her jacket from the back of the chair and slipped out into the hallway.

Clearly the change in her was noticeable to others besides just her. She needed to leave. To get away.

She scanned the hall and made the quick decision to take the exit out of the back of the hospital. It was a small building and if she went through the front, no doubt she'd run into everyone else. She couldn't risk it.

Bree kept her head down and moved quickly. She held her breath until she finally pushed out the glass door that would lead her to the parking lot and—

"Hey there."

A mixture of excitement and terror flashed through her simultaneously. The only thing Bree had time to think before she opened her eyes and saw the man standing in front of her was, *I'm in so much trouble.*

LIAM HAD ASSUMED that a few days apart from Bree might have helped ease whatever it was he was feeling for her.

He was wrong.

Those feelings had only intensified.

The moment she stepped outside, his bear had gone wild.

She was near.

Lucky for him, he hadn't gone inside with the others, but had decided to go for a little walk to clear his head first. Besides, with everyone else there to see Kira and the babies, he was pretty sure his cousin wouldn't notice his absence. And babies weren't really his thing.

Not yet.

It was a ludicrous thought and one that he had no business entertaining at all. He'd never once considered having cubs of his own. Of course he'd never met his…what *was* she?

Liam had forced the thought out of his head the moment it came in. He didn't have time to think about such ridiculous things. Not when he had a woman to find. And a whole lot to get to the bottom of when it came to that woman. Because with every second that went by, Liam became more and more certain that there was something Bree wasn't telling him.

Something important.

"Hey there."

Startled, Bree had spun around and clutched a hand to her chest.

He hadn't meant to scare her. In fact, he'd been almost certain she'd seen him, but judging by the fear in her eyes, that was clearly not the case.

"I'm sorry," Liam said quickly. He held up his hands. "I didn't mean to frighten you."

Slowly, she dropped her hand to her side and shook her head. "You didn't," she lied. "I was just thinking about…" She looked around quickly. "I really need to get going."

He grabbed Bree's arm before she could slip away. Even through the thick wool of her coat, he could feel her heat, and it shot right through him. What he wouldn't give to feel her skin against his again.

Soon.

"How's Kira? The babies?" He'd already heard, along with the others, that the delivery had gone smoothly and very quickly, and mother and babies were resting comfortably. But it seemed like the right thing to ask.

"They're good." Her mouth split into a genuine smile. "They're doing amazing and the babies are so cute. They haven't named them yet. I think they're waiting until…well, you should probably get in there. They were hoping to have all the family—"

"You're family."

Her smile fell. "No," she said softly. "I'm not. And I'm sorry, Liam. But I really need to get—"

"Don't go."

He stepped closer. The need to be near her pulled him. She opened her mouth to say something, but closed it again and took a deep breath instead.

"Bree." Liam moved closer still. It was as if there were a magnet drawing them together. He couldn't control it even if he wanted to.

And he most certainly did not want to.

She lifted her eyes to meet his and before he could stop himself, Liam kissed her. His mouth was on hers. Tasting her. Feeling her. His hands came up to cup her head and the frigid cold around them was completely forgotten for the heat the two of them put off.

He could have kissed her all day. Hell, he could have done a lot more than that. But as quickly as the kiss started, it was over.

Bree pushed him away and touched her fingers to her lips. "I can't do this."

"Yes." He traced a finger down her cheek. "You can. There's something…" He shook his head, unsure how to put into words what he was feeling. "There's something about you, Bree. Something I don't think you even understand."

She squeezed her eyes shut, but not before he caught a flash of something in them.

What was she hiding?

"Come with me." Liam took her hand and threaded his fingers through hers.

"Where?"

"Back to Grizzly Ridge. Harper wants to hold the first event soon and—"

"No." She shook her head. "I can't. I can't do that anymore. It was a bad idea. I need to…I just can't, Liam." Tears pooled in her eyes.

What was going on with this woman?

"Bree. Talk to me."

His bear was going crazy. His instincts were blurry and clouded, but there was something off and he'd be damned if he wasn't going to get to the bottom of it. Although, for the life of him, Liam couldn't have told anyone who asked why it was so important that he understand anything about this human woman except that…it was instinct. He *had* to know what was going on.

"I can't, Liam." Tears spilled from her eyes and streaked her cheeks as she spoke a flurry of words. "It's not that easy. I never should have been with you the other night. It was a mistake and I never should have let you…I shouldn't have…it's my…it never should have happened. Everything is different now. It changed—"

"Yes." He interrupted her. "It absolutely should have happened. A hundred times, yes, Bree. And you know it." He tipped her head up so she would look at him. He stared into the depth of her green eyes and that's when he saw it. She *was* changed. *She was—*

"Bree?" Liam took a step back. "Who are you exactly?"

Confusion and fear crossed her face and she tried to move away, but Liam held her fast.

"No," he tried again. "*What* are you?"

SHE COULD HAVE FOUGHT him off, slipped out of his arms and run.

But run to…*where*? She was no longer sure. Besides, she was tired of running and it was getting too hard to keep up the story.

Bree slumped against the cold stone wall of the hospital and confessed. "I'm a grizzly shifter."

It was the first time that she could remember ever saying the words out loud. Even as a child, she'd never said it. Not once. Hell, she'd hardly even known the truth about herself. She'd been so young when her parents died. When they were taken from her and her whole life had jumped track.

If you lived a lie for long enough, it would finally become your truth. And until she said the words out loud and felt them on her tongue, her life as a human *had* been her truth.

But not anymore.

"What?" Liam tilted his head, but despite his question, he didn't look surprised. "A grizzly?"

She nodded.

"How? When? Why?"

"I assume the same way you're a shifter," she said with a sly smile, unable to resist the sarcasm. "Always and…I don't really know how to answer that question."

Liam shook his head. "Okay, wrong questions," he admitted with a smile. "But…" He took a step back and looked around him briefly before tugging on her hand. "Come on. Let's get out of the cold."

She couldn't argue with that.

"Let's go to my place."

"No." He shook his head. "I need to take you to the ridge. It'll be safer."

"Safer?" A trail of ice ran down her spine, and it had nothing to do with the frigid temperatures. *Did he know who she was? Did he know who her clan was? What they'd done? Would they find her? Would Liam turn her in? Was she—*

"Absolutely," Liam said. "It's not going to get any warmer. And if your heater goes out the way ours did up at the ridge last night, you'd freeze before anyone could get down to help you. Besides, it's forecasted to snow again and the plow is giving us trouble." He wrapped an arm around her shoulders, and Bree instinctively leaned into him. In that moment, she felt safer than she could ever remember.

"Okay."

They didn't speak for the entire drive back to the ridge. Liam focused intently on the icy road. Bree absentmindedly spun the ring on her finger and passed the time staring out the window at the snow-covered world. Decembers were always snowy and cold in Montana, but this year had been different. They'd already had more snow than usual. Not that she minded. Not really. Bree liked the snow. Well, except driving in it. But with Liam behind the wheel, navigating them competently back to the ridge, she felt safe.

Safe.

There it was again. That feeling of being protected and taken care of and...she almost laughed out loud at herself.

She was a strong woman. Hell, she was a grizzly, even if she'd never admitted it—even to herself. She was born to be a strong woman. She didn't need a man to take care of her, protect her, or keep her safe. She could do that all on her own, thank you very much—shifter or not.

Bree snuck a glance at Liam.

Still. It's nice.

It was. She couldn't deny that. Something about having Liam close to her felt good. It didn't matter that they weren't talking or touching. Just his presence calmed her.

The ridge was quiet. The buildings were deserted because everyone had made their way down into town to see Kira, Nash, and the twins.

They had the place to themselves, which helped ease any remaining nerves Bree had about what she was about to tell Liam. Because she'd already made the decision to tell him the truth. She trusted him, and really, she trusted the rest of the Jacksons, too. But…that little flicker of doubt was always there. *What if the wrong person heard her story? What if, after all of this time, all of her hiding, everything her grandparents had been through, she wasn't safe anymore?*

Chapter Nine

A GRIZZLY.

A shifter.

Liam still couldn't believe it. She'd said the words, and as much as they made sense in his head the moment she'd said them, at the same time, nothing made sense.

How come he hadn't been able to sense it? How had no one been able to sense it?

The woman had been surrounded by grizzly shifters and not one of them knew the truth? It seemed impossible. It *had* to be impossible.

But yet…he'd sensed that something was different with her. *Especially after they'd…*

He finished stoking the fire and turned back to look at her. She had her back turned to him, so Liam had a few moments to watch her.

The attraction he had for her had been intense from the start. *No.* More than intense. It had been absolutely unmatched. From the moment he laid eyes on her, he had to have her. But it wasn't until after they'd been together that everything had really changed. That's when his bear had *really* started to react to her.

Could it be…could she *be…*

Bree turned around and walked toward him.

He gestured to the couch and handed her a blanket. "It's still pretty chilly in here," he said. "The fire will warm things up, but until then…"

"Thanks." She took it and wrapped herself in a cocoon before sitting cross-legged on the couch.

He sat next to her, facing her but not touching. As much as he wanted to hold her and feel her against him, Liam knew that she'd need space to tell him whatever it was she was about to reveal.

"So," she started. "I guess you have a few questions."

He couldn't help it; Liam chuckled. "You could say that. I have quite a few questions. But mostly I just want to hear your story, Bree. I promise whatever it is you need to say, your secret is safe with me. Do you trust me?"

She nodded without hesitation. "I do."

Liam waited while Bree looked down, took a deep breath, and then looked up and started speaking. "My mother's name was Lucy. My father was Brendan. My mother was the only daughter of the Sterling clan from Colorado. The Sterling clan, like so many other grizzly clans, have—or have had— some pretty traditional rules when it comes to mates." He nodded. He knew all about that. "Of course, my mother was promised to the son of another clan member and…"

"This sounds familiar." Liam smiled sympathetically. "Were they exiled?" It wouldn't surprise him. After all, that's what had happened to his cousins when Kira chose an *unsuitable* mate and of course to their mother before them. It really was a running theme for grizzly clans. Liam had come around to the new way of thinking a little later than the rest. But he was there now. Mostly.

Bree pressed her lips together and shook her head. "Not exactly."

Liam tipped his head and waited.

"They ran," she said after a moment. "Her family made no secret that her choice of mate wouldn't be tolerated. Not even in exile. So they ran off." Her face took on a faraway look and despite the seriousness of what they were discussing, her lips twitched up in a small smile. "I like to think of them back then," she said after a moment. "So young. So in love. They didn't care what anyone else said. They were going to be together. And they were, for a few years. They went south, to a town where no one knew them. As far as they knew, there were no other shifters in the area. They changed their names, and had me.

"For a while, I think life was pretty good. They didn't have a lot. But what they did have was theirs and they were together. That was all that mattered." Bree's eyes shone with unshed tears, but she kept talking. "I'm not sure how, but somehow the Raymonds, an elderly couple who lived next door, found out who they really were. But they didn't care and they promised to keep my parents' secret. They became part of our family and for as long as I could remember, they were always there for all the things. And for the thing that really mattered."

Bree closed her eyes and took a breath.

"It's okay," Liam said, although he had no idea whether it was or not. "Tell me what happened."

She nodded. "It was right after my fifth birthday. Mom had just finished tucking me into bed when I heard them. They smashed through the front door. I could hear voices. Yelling. Fighting. And then my mom screaming. I snuck out of bed and peeked down the hall and that's when I saw my dad."

Bree closed her eyes again, but kept talking. Liam moved closer on the couch and took her hands in his while she spoke.

"He was covered in blood, but I could see his eyes. I'll

never forget them. I'll never forget the way his eyes seemed to tell me to run. He never said a word. But it was in his eyes." Bree looked at him then. "Does that make sense?"

"It does. Shifters have an innate way of communicating to each other. Especially in times of heightened emotion or crisis. It makes perfect sense." He squeezed her hands gently, in a way he hoped was reassuring. "So where did you run?"

"To the Raymonds'. To my grandparents."

TELLING Liam the story of what had happened wasn't nearly as scary as Bree thought it would be. She'd never before talked about the events of that night. Not even with her grandparents. Not really. They'd talked about it once, when she was eleven or twelve and started remembering things. They filled in the gaps for her, and the story became complete. But it didn't make it any easier. And they wouldn't talk about it again. Not really. It felt good to finally get it all out and say it out loud.

"They didn't seem surprised to see me," Bree continued. "My grandpa already had some bags in the car, as if they'd already packed. I remember being confused and thinking they were going on a trip. And then I was excited for a second because I got to go with them. But then I remembered my dad on the floor and the blood and the sound of my mother's screams."

"Bree, I'm so…"

Liam pulled her into his arms and held her tight, but the tears that had been threatening to fall, didn't. It had been a long time ago. She'd been so young. She barely even remembered her parents. Liam rubbed her back and murmured in her ear, and she let herself lean into it. His care and concern for her infused her and gave her a renewed strength to continue.

"It's okay." She pulled back and offered him a smile. "It really is."

"So, where did you go? I assume your *grandparents* helped you get away."

"We came here." Bree shrugged. "Later, they told me that my mom had started to worry that the Sterling clan had somehow gotten wind of where they were. My dad kept telling her not to worry, but my mom, she knew her brothers. And they weren't the type to give up so easily."

"Wait." Liam stopped her. "It was her brothers who found you? Her brothers who—"

"Killed them." She nodded. "Yes."

"Wow." Liam shook his head in disbelief. "I couldn't imagine. Even with everything that happened…I never meant to hurt Natalia." His eyes clouded with concern. "I would never have—"

"I know you wouldn't have hurt her." Bree knew that now more than ever. After the fight Nat and Liam had, Natalia had been seriously injured, but his sister had always believed that Liam hadn't meant to take it that far. And now that Bree knew him the way she did, she knew it too. Liam never would have behaved the way her own clan had.

Her clan.

It felt strange to think of it that way after all this time.

"Anyway," she forced herself to finish her story, "my mom had put the Raymonds on alert and made them promise to keep me safe and start over somewhere. She made them promise to never let me know that side of myself."

"Your shifter side?" Liam's face lined with confusion. "I don't understand. How did you…"

She held up a finger. "One thing at a time."

Liam nodded, although she could see he had more and more questions to ask her.

"They brought me here," she said. "And they raised me like

a normal girl. When I became a teenager, they had to tell me more. They sat me down and told me about shifters and who I was. It kind of became a necessity." She laughed because every shifter knew that the hardest time for a shifter was when you went through puberty and your bear started to wake up. Hormones were hard enough to deal with, but when you were dealing with a hormonal bear deep inside that you didn't understand, well, angst didn't even begin to describe how difficult it could be.

Most young shifters solved the problem by embracing their animal and undergoing the first shift. After that, the animal inside calmed and over time, a teenage shifter could learn how to control their bear and even harness the strength and power it gave them.

But if you never experienced that first shift, the powers and instincts, and even the pheromones that a shifter put out, all diminished. The longer you denied your bear, the more muted it became.

"Once they explained everything," Bree continued, "they also explained the danger and that if I ever acknowledged the bear side of myself, I'd be putting myself in grave danger. They told me that as soon as I became a full grizzly shifter, my clan would know. They'd know how to find me and…" She let the thought trail away.

"So how did you manage it?" Liam asked. "How did you handle that first shift? It's a hard one and—"

"I didn't."

"You what?" Liam sat back and stared at her.

"I didn't shift."

"Ever?"

She shook her head.

"How?" He released one hand and scrubbed it across his face, as if that would help him make sense of what she was saying. "If you didn't have that first shift...wait! That's how you did it!"

Bree couldn't help it. Nothing about what they were talking about was funny. But, she laughed. "Yes," she said after a moment. "That's how I did it." She shrugged. "Whatever *it* is."

LIAM JUMPED TO HIS FEET. He needed to process what she'd just said.

Bree was a shifter.

Her parents had been killed by her mother's clan.

She'd fled.

She'd never shifted.

She'd denied her bear.

She was...*hibernating*?

He paced in front of the fire for a moment, letting it all sink in.

Liam turned to ask her a question, but it died on his lips. He swallowed and turned back to his pacing for another minute.

Finally, he'd worked through it all in his head.

"You've never shifted?" he asked again as he stood in front of her on the couch. "Not once?"

She shook her head the way he knew she would.

"That's how no one ever sensed it before. That's how you've managed to be able to hide in plain sight."

She nodded. "And no one ever looked very closely," she added. "When you tell someone something, they want to believe it."

"And why would anyone have ever thought not to believe that you were who you said you were?" Liam nodded as he put all the pieces together. "Of course."

He sat on the couch again, his body turned to her. "But

that doesn't explain the way I reacted to you the first time I saw you. And then…"

She blushed. He didn't have to ask to know she felt exactly the same way he did about her. And now it all made sense. *Perfect sense.*

"We're mates," he blurted out. "Fated mates."

Bree shook her head and jumped up from the couch. For a moment, Liam thought she might run for the door, but she stopped and wrapped her arms around her body. Her breasts pushed up against the thin blouse she wore. "No. That's not possible."

"It's not only possible." He stood in front of her. "It *is.*" He reached for her and held her gently by the shoulders. "You're my mate, Bree. We're fated. It's the only explanation for every-thing. The way I've been drawn to you since the first time I saw you. The way you've gotten in my head."

Slowly, she dropped her arms.

"And when we were…" Liam tucked a stray strand of hair behind her ear and cupped her cheek. "When we were together, it opened something inside me. And I feel it from you, too. Something changed inside you."

She squeezed her eyes shut, and the tears finally slipped down her cheeks.

"I could sense it right away," Liam continued.

It all made sense now. The way she'd reacted after they'd made love. The way she'd kicked him out of her house so abruptly. It was so he wouldn't have time to notice the change in her. So he wouldn't be able to sense her bear. Because when they were together, it had awoken her bear.

Because he was her mate.

His bear knew it. And now her bear knew it too.

"You're awake," he whispered. "Your bear."

She wouldn't look at him, but she nodded.

Carefully, Liam reached out and wiped the tears from her

cheeks, but they continued to fall. "Why are you crying, babe? This is a good thing. Denying your bear must have been so hard and now that she's—"

"No."

Bree looked up and for the first time, Liam noticed the fear in her eyes. Genuine fear. His heart clenched and his bear roared. Whatever or *whomever* it was that his mate was scared of, he knew he'd never let anything happen to her. Ever.

"I can't let it happen, Liam." Bree's voice shook as she continued to cry. "I can't let my bear out. I can't...it's not safe. What if—"

"I will never let anything happen to you, Bree." He cupped her face in his hands and stared directly into her beautiful eyes, willing her to believe him. "Ever."

He pressed his lips to hers in a kiss that he hoped conveyed everything that he felt for her so there was no more room for confusion of any kind. Because, in the last few minutes, everything had become crystal-clear for Liam. They were fated.

And no matter what the risk was, he was willing to take it. Now he just needed to convince her.

Chapter Ten

SHE WANTED TO BELIEVE HIM. More than anything, Bree wanted to believe that she'd be safe. But…what if she wasn't? What if now that her bear was *awake,* they found her? *What if they tracked her down and…*

She sat back against the couch, her tears still wet on her cheek, and stared straight ahead. "It's too much," she said after a moment. "I just wanted to live my life and everything was going so…" She turned to look at him, and her heart did a crazy flip in her chest. Now that she'd met him, she couldn't take it back. She couldn't turn back time to before they'd met.

And more than that, she didn't want to.

Mates?

Fated mates?

Bree didn't know about all of that. But Liam was right about one thing…now that her bear was awake, there was no way she was going back to sleep. Bree knew that in her heart. As a teenager, it had been difficult to shut down the animal that lived inside her. But not impossible. Now that her bear had met Liam, had experienced that closeness with him, there was absolutely no way.

"One step at a time, babe." Liam took her hand and looked straight into her eyes. "This is all still so new to you. I mean, you've never even…"

"Shifted?"

Liam shook his head. "I still can't believe that."

"Believe it."

"It must have been so hard."

She laughed. "It was at first. But then it got easier, and then…well, I guess I finally convinced myself that it wasn't a thing and you can't miss what you've never known."

"You are the strongest woman I've ever met, Bree." Liam's eyes widened with awe and respect. "The strength and discipline it must have taken to deny yourself that way. It's unbelievable. Never mind all the other stuff you've been through. It's incredible."

"I don't know about that." Bree could feel the heat in her cheeks rising.

"I do." Liam jumped to his feet. "And that's how I know you're going to be okay with this, too."

She eyed him cautiously. "What's *this?*"

"Do you trust me?"

She did. Completely. She nodded slightly and he extended a hand down to her.

She took it and he pulled her gently to her feet. "It's long past time you met your bear."

The idea filled her with a cold panic that made her instinctively pull back, but Liam held her hand tight. "You got this, Bree. You can do it."

"I can't." She shook her head, but allowed him to lead her across the room. "I don't know how."

"That's the beauty of it." Liam's smile was genuine and reassuring. "You just let your bear do the work. Because the thing is, you *do* know what to do. It's instinct."

She still didn't believe him. Not completely. The whole idea seemed so totally foreign that it was just impossible. She squeezed her eyes shut and took a deep breath as Liam turned her in his arms.

He kissed her and just as it happened every time, something deep inside her sparked to life. It started low in her gut, and quickly traveled through her veins to every part of her until she felt as though she were vibrating.

Bree threaded her fingers through Liam's thick hair and deepened the kiss. She pulled her body into his hard chest and groaned. It was a sound unlike anything she'd heard before. And it came from her.

With a jolt of surprise, Bree tried to pull back, but Liam held her firm.

"What was..."

"That was your bear. Let it go. Let yourself feel it. Feel everything."

Liam trailed his hands down her back, to the hem of her sweater. Before she realized what he was doing, he lifted it up and over her head. Her hair fanned out over her bare back and she brought her arms up to cover herself.

"What are you doing?" She looked around frantically, but there was no one there. Everyone was still down in town, and no doubt would be for a while. But still, she said, "We can't do this here."

"Yes." He smiled. "We can. Besides, you don't want to ruin your clothes. That would be hard to explain, wouldn't it?"

Ruin my...

Her eyes widened as she put together exactly what he was saying.

"You don't mean that I should...you think I should...I don't even know if I can."

"Shift?" Liam nodded and moved his fingers to the button of her jeans. "You can. I have no doubt of that. Your bear is right here, babe. She's right at the surface." Liam pushed her jeans down and she wiggled out of them until she stood in front of him in only her bra and panties. "You're gorgeous. I can't wait to see all of you."

"You have seen all of me." The bashfulness of only a moment before had vanished, replaced by a strength she could feel that came from somewhere deep inside.

"And you're the most beautiful woman I've ever seen." He teased at the edge of her bra with his thumb. "But your bear... I can't wait to see her."

SHE TRUSTED HIM. Liam could see it in her eyes and the responsibility of what that meant made his heart swell.

With every moment that passed, his feelings for Bree grew stronger. But when he took her hand and led her outside into the cold air, he was completely unprepared for how much stronger those feelings would get in only an instant.

He kissed her again, cutting off her protests about the cold. This time when he kissed her, he let his hands travel down her body to the hot cleft between her legs. She was already wet for him through the lace of her panties, but she was still too tense. Thinking too much.

And there was one way he knew to make her *think* a lot less and *feel* a lot more.

Liam slipped one finger under the elastic and circled her hard nub. She sighed and her knees buckled with the attention, but he held her fast and deepened his kiss as he pressed deep inside her. She let out a gasp that turned into a moan.

It wouldn't take long.

Liam hooked his finger up to press on the sensitive spot deep inside her that he knew would make her come undone. Just as he knew she would, Bree shuddered. Her body responded immediately to his attentions.

It was time.

He pulled away from her and her eyes snapped open in question.

"Feel her," Liam said. "Feel your bear and just let go."

Bree nodded and turned her back to him. She stood at the edge of the porch and looked out over the snowy field where only a few hours ago the helicopter had landed. Just beyond that were the thick trees between them and the ridge.

She turned and looked back at him.

Liam nodded and then it happened.

Bree moved so swiftly, so gracefully as she trusted in her bear and herself and leapt from the porch.

The transformation was beautiful and easy, and by the time she landed on the ground a moment later, a strong, beautiful grizzly had replaced his soft, curvy Bree.

She was stunning.

Liam made short work of his own clothes, tossing them on a chair behind him before he ran and jumped off the porch. He was so used to shifting, he barely had to think about it. But he knew it would be a bit more challenging for Bree. At least at first.

He also knew they wouldn't have long for this first shift. It took stamina to be in your bear. They'd have to work up to it.

Liam joined her on the ground and as much as he wanted to take a second look at her, and a third and maybe even a fourth, the moment his feet hit the ground, he started running. With his mate at his side.

Ready for this?

Bree broke her stride, just a little, as his thought settled in her mind, but it was just a second before she responded.

More than anything.

Together, they increased their speed and in an instant were across the field and into the cover of the trees. Bree took to it immediately, not that he had any doubt about it. As soon as she told him her story, Liam had known that as soon as she embraced her bear, everything would change. And for that moment, that meant letting Bree experience the pure freedom and joy of running with your animal.

There was nothing quite like connecting with that other part of yourself. It couldn't be explained to anyone who hadn't experienced it. But once you knew for yourself what it was like to shift and connect with your animal, there was no going back. It was as if a whole other part of yourself opened up.

Liam could sense that in Bree. He didn't even have to look at her to know what she was experiencing. She wouldn't be the same after this. How could she be?

He steered them toward the ridge. The snow wasn't as deep in the trees, but the passage was still more challenging than he would have liked. Liam knew they wouldn't have long for this first shift but he was determined to get her to the ridge. To take in the glory that was the valley below, and the peaks of the mountains in the distance was something that couldn't be matched. Of course, she'd seen it before as a human. But this was different.

They burst through a stand of trees and there it was.

Next to him, Bree slowed and came to a stop. She sat and he moved back to join her.

Amazing, isn't it?

She moved her head, taking it all in.

It is. All of it.

Her gaze landed on him.

Thank you.

Chapter Eleven

BREE WAS both exhausted and exhilarated all at once. They hadn't been out for very long, but when they returned to the Den, and she'd shifted back, the exhaustion had settled over her almost at once.

Liam had insisted on scooping her up and carrying her up to his bed in the guest room. Not that she was protesting. Being in his arms was something Bree was pretty sure she would never protest.

It felt good.

Really good.

He'd tucked her in and crawled into the bed with her. Despite how tired she was, his nearness lit a fire deep inside her and she wiggled back against him, fully prepared to take the cuddle to the next level.

"Let's finish what we started earlier."

But Liam only chuckled and wrapped his arms tighter around her. He kissed the back of her neck and whispered in her ear. "There'll be plenty of time for that later, I promise. For now, sleep. You need to recharge."

Bree wanted to protest again. She wanted to insist that she wasn't tired and she had lots of energy. But before she could even open her mouth to tell him, she was asleep.

When she woke up hours later, the room was dark, and she was alone.

But she didn't *feel* alone. Quite the opposite.

She raised her arms over her head and slowly stretched each of her muscles. Testing them for soreness. And they were sore. Her entire body ached, but it felt good. Like she'd just been through a tough workout. Which, in a way, she had.

She marveled at how easily her body had responded to her bear. She'd expected it to be hard. Painful, even. But it was neither of those things. Instead, it felt like the most natural thing in the world to let her bear take over.

How have I lived this long without it?

She'd denied herself for the last time. Because not only had it felt amazing to shift, the internal calm she felt now was even better.

Slowly, Bree moved from the bed and found her clothes neatly folded on the dresser. She smiled at Liam's thoughtfulness.

Even though he wasn't in the room, he was close by. She could feel it.

Was that because he was her mate?

Mate!

The idea seemed both completely ludicrous and totally right all at the same time.

She'd blocked out her true self for so long, that she'd never even allowed herself to think about having someone in her life. Let alone a mate. But Liam…despite the short time she'd known him, she couldn't imagine her life without him.

The very thought, no matter how fleeting, caused a tightness in her chest. A shortness of breath.

No.

She wouldn't live without him. She knew that in her gut.

My mate.

Bree dressed and slipped out of the room into the hall. Voices traveled up the stairs from the great room below. *Everyone must be back from the hospital.*

The sweet smell of cookies and icing drifted up to her, and her stomach growled.

She was only halfway down the stairs when Liam came to join her.

"Good morning, sunshine." He kissed her forehead and took her hand.

"What time is it? You should have woke me."

"Are you kidding? You needed to rest. Besides, it gave me a chance to fill everyone in on what happened."

Bree froze and spun to face him. "You told them? How could you do that?" She glanced down the stairs, but no one was looking at them. The sounds of laughter and Christmas carols floated up to her.

Liam squeezed her hands and forced her attention back to him. "I had to, Bree. Besides, they would have figured it out. You're different. You can't hide it anymore."

Was she different?

She knew the answer.

She was. She was *very* different. Fundamentally changed. She could feel it and Liam was right. They'd be able to sense it. The fact that she'd been able to hide it for so long was impressive. If she thought things had changed after she'd had sex with Liam, there was no way she could keep hiding it now that she'd shifted.

She nodded. "Okay."

"It *is* okay, Bree. It really is. Everyone loves you. We're not going to let anything happen to you. There's really nothing to worry about. I promise."

She wanted to believe him. But despite how much she trusted him and how much she *wanted* to believe him, she couldn't shake the fear. The Sterling clan had killed her parents. She had no reason to believe that they wouldn't kill her, too. After all, she was the product of their union. If they hated it so much, surely they would hate her.

"Stop overthinking." Liam shook her from her thoughts. "You're safe, Bree. Really, you are. I promise. Do you believe me?"

After a moment, she nodded. "I do."

LIAM WASN'T sure whether she did completely or not. But she would. She trusted him and that's all that mattered. Because he meant every word of what he'd said. She had nothing to worry about. He would bet his life on it.

"Let's stop worrying," he said. "At least for tonight, okay? I need you downstairs." He gestured to the festivities taking place. "I'm getting my ass kicked in cookie decorating." He laughed. "Please tell me you have some skills in this area."

She smiled. It lit up her entire face and in that moment, Liam vowed to do whatever it took to keep that smile on her face forever.

"Baby, I have all kinds of skills you haven't seen yet."

His groin twitched and his cock thickened in anticipation of learning exactly what skills she was talking about. But it would have to wait because he hadn't been lying when he said he was getting his ass handed to him in cookie decorating.

And although the Reindeer Games were supposed to be just for fun, when you had a room full of alphas, all with a very competitive streak, even cookie decorating could become cutthroat.

Bree was greeted with hugs and smiles from everyone in the

room. They truly did love her. When Liam had explained what was going on, everyone had been surprised. Everyone but Kade. Apparently when Bree had been with Kira in the hospital, Kira had noticed something different about their friend and of course, despite the fact that Kira more than had her hands full with the birth of her cubs, she couldn't get it out of her head. Which meant, Kade, as her twin, had picked up on his sister's concern.

Still, no one had expected the story that Liam had relayed to them. They were shocked, and maybe even a little hurt that Bree hadn't confided in them. He knew they'd get past any lingering hurt, because that's who the Jacksons were. They loved hard and protected their own. And Bree was their own.

There'd be lots of time to talk about next steps in the coming days. But for now, Liam had been serious about focusing on the competition.

He led her to the end of the table where he'd set up his decorating station and pulled out a chair for her. But Bree wasn't interested in sitting. She picked up a Christmas tree-shaped cookie and held it up.

"What is this?"

"A Christmas tree."

She raised an eyebrow. "Are you sure? Because it kind of looks like a....well, I actually don't know what it looks like."

Liam laughed. "I told you—I need you."

He needed her in so many other ways, but he also knew he'd have to settle for just cookie decorating for the moment.

"Do you ever." She shook her head and took a bite of the cookie.

"Hey! We need that!"

"We do not need this," she said with a mouthful. "Except it really is delicious." She grinned. "Pass me the icing. Let's do this."

For the next thirty minutes, Liam acted as Bree's assistant.

He fetched icing, sprinkles, and other adornments of all kinds. Mostly he sat in awe as she wielded piping bags and other tools that he had no idea existed.

"Time is almost up," Harper announced from the front of the room. "Judging will start soon. Finish up your last cookie."

"We need a nose!" Bree spun so quickly, a stream of white icing shot out of the tube she was holding and landed on Liam's face. "Whoops."

He laughed and wiped it from his cheek before licking the sugary confection from his finger. "Delicious."

Bree leaned in and kissed him. She took her time before leaning back and licking her lips. "It certainly is."

Damn.

Once again, Liam's cock stiffened. The cookie decorating couldn't be finished soon enough, as far as he was concerned. He needed to get his mate alone.

"We need a nose," Bree said again, pulling his attention back to the situation at hand.

"A nose?"

She gestured to the cookie she'd been working on. It was a reindeer shape and miraculously—because, unlike him, Bree actually had skills—it *looked* like a reindeer. At least it would as soon as it had a nose.

"Just use the icing."

"No." She shook her head. "We need a great nose." She scanned the table that was littered with candies of all kinds. "That one!" She pointed to a mini red jawbreaker. "It'll be Rudolph."

Liam reached across the table and plucked the candy from the mess moments before Cyrus reached for the same one.

"Sorry, man." Liam shrugged. "All's fair in cookie decorating."

Cyrus growled, but it was all in fun and with a triumphant

grin, Liam stuck the *nose* on the cookie only seconds before Harper announced that time was up.

Bree sat back with a satisfied smile on her face. "That was fun. But I didn't expect—hey!"

Liam interrupted her with a swipe of icing across her face. Stunned for a moment, she didn't react. But it only lasted a moment before she picked up a handful of the sprinkles on the table in front of her and tossed them at Liam.

"You didn't just do that." He shook his head and bits of candy fell from his hair.

"I most certainly did." She laughed and it was game on.

Cyrus, Natalia, Chloe, Zoe, and Luke all joined in on the icing and candy fight while the others retreated to a safe distance. All except Harper, who risked herself getting bombed with candy long enough to save the plates of prepared cookies.

Liam dodged around Cyrus and grabbed a piping bag full of icing before chasing Bree around the table. He finally caught her, wrapped her up in his arms, and, instead of squirting her with the icing, pulled her in for a long kiss. Because there was no icing in the world sweeter than the taste of her mouth on his.

His bear growled deep inside. He needed to make her his.

Completely uncaring that they were standing in the middle of the living room, they would have continued to kiss all night, or more, if it hadn't been for Natalia yelling at them to break it up.

"This is a family show." She laughed. "Seriously," Nat said when they did move apart. "As thrilled as I am for whatever this is that's going on here," she gestured between them, "there are cookies to judge."

"Exactly." Harper gave Liam a chastising look, but he only shrugged. "I'll go find Ella and Kade while you guys clean this up. They were just here." She let out a deep sigh. "Don't tell me that they snuck off to make out, too." She shook her head as Axel wrapped his arms around her from behind.

"We could sneak off, too…"

She swatted his arm playfully and everyone laughed because it was definitely the one thing they all had in common —the undeniable draw to all of their mates.

And now Liam had it, too.

Chapter Twelve

"I STILL THINK we should have won," Bree said the next morning. After locating Ella and Kade, who had only retreated as far as the kitchen to make a cup of tea, they'd subjected their cookies to judging.

Bree couldn't help but notice how tired Ella looked as she judged the cookies, but she didn't say anything and it was soon forgotten anyway as Ella announced Zoe and Gabe as the winners of the first event.

Not that it had mattered all that much, because as soon as the judging was over, Liam had all but swept her off her feet and ran upstairs with her, where they'd made love all through the night.

If she thought her muscles were sore before, she'd taken things to a whole new level. Every part of her ached in the most delicious way, because the best kind of body ache was the kind that came from a night of passionate lovemaking.

"Baby, I've already won." Liam traced a finger down her arm to dip below the quilt that barely covered her cleavage. In response, Bree wiggled closer to him. She pushed the blanket off them both, so she could see him properly before running both her hands over his hard chest and down to his hips. He was already hard for her.

Again.

Liam seemed to have an unending reserve of energy. Bree didn't have a lot of experience with men, but she did know that they generally needed a recovery time between sessions.

Not Liam.

He was always ready to go. It both impressed her and turned her on.

Bree pushed him to his back and climbed up so she straddled him. His eyes widened with appreciation as he looked up at her. "Now that's the kind of view I like in the morning. Damn, baby. You're so sexy."

Never in her life had Bree felt sexy. Not like this. Sure, she'd dressed up and felt good before. But this was different.

The way Liam looked at her with nothing but pure appreciation in his eyes…the way he wanted her, and didn't make any effort to hide it, was the greatest turn-on in the world.

She wiggled a little and Liam's hands clamped down on her hips. "You're going to be the death of me, woman."

"Seems like a good way to go." She bent down and kissed him, sucking on his bottom lip before sitting up again.

"I can't think of a better way." With a strength she still couldn't believe, he lifted her a little and brought her back down on his hard rod.

She groaned as he filled her completely. He held her in place for a moment before she started moving.

"I lied," he said. "This would be the best way to go." He looked her straight in the eyes. "With you on my cock."

The corner of her mouth twitched up in a little grin. She felt powerful and strong and sexy.

"I love you, Bree."

She nodded. "I know."

He laughed. "I know it seems crazy."

"It doesn't." She shook her head a little but didn't slow her movements. "I love you, too."

From the bottom of her heart, she meant it. She *did* love him. In a whole body, totally consuming way that she couldn't even begin to explain. It should have seemed insane to fall so completely and totally in love with someone you'd only met a few days earlier, but it wasn't. It wasn't insane at all. Her soul knew he was hers, and she was his. It was the most natural thing in the whole world.

"You're mine."

"I'm yours," she agreed. "And you're mine."

In a flash, he moved and Bree was under him. Still inside her, Liam loomed over her. Passion and love flared in his eyes. "I need you, Bree."

"You have me."

"No." His tone was serious. "I *need* to make you mine."

Her body stiffened slightly as she realized what he meant. "You mean like…"

He nodded. "I need to take you as my mate."

Liam waited. She knew he wanted an answer. But not just any answer. He wanted her to say yes. That of course she wanted him as her mate just as much as he wanted her.

And maybe she did.

But it was too soon. There had already been so many changes that she could barely keep up. She'd only met Liam a few days ago, for goodness' sake, and now…a *mate?* That was for life. That was serious. A commitment.

It was what got her parents killed.

"Bree?"

She squeezed her eyes shut. She couldn't breathe. It felt as if she were suffocating under him and she couldn't get a full breath.

"Bree?"

She shook her head from side to side. Just a little at first, and then with more urgency.

"No." The word slipped from between her lips, barely more than a whisper.

"What?" Liam pushed up and off her.

"No," she said again, this time looking in his eyes.

NO?

She'd said no.

It felt as if he'd been punched in the chest. *How could she say no? She was his. He was hers. It didn't make sense. And there was no way he was going to let her go. No way.* Despite it being the last thing he wanted to do, Liam forced himself not to react.

"No?"

Bree sat up. "I'm sorry, Liam." She shook her head. "I can't. It's too much. Not right now."

Of course.

It really *was* too much. At least it would be for her. Up until yesterday, she hadn't even accepted her bear; how could he reasonably expect her to jump into the deep end of shifter life?

He reached out, needing to have a connection with her, and twined his fingers in hers. "But this…" He pointed with one finger between them. "We…you and…well, I guess what I'm trying to say is…"

"Yes." She laughed and sat up cross-legged on the bed in front of him. "If you're asking if me and you can still be a *thing*," she held her fingers up in quotes, "the answer is absolutely a yes." Her smile dipped for a moment. "That is, if you still want that."

He couldn't think of anything else in the entire world that he wanted more.

Except being her mate.

But that would have to wait.

Not forever. But for the moment.

He wasn't normally a patient man. He wanted what he wanted, when he wanted it. But Bree…she was worth waiting for.

Especially because in the meantime, he would happily take what he could get with her. He didn't even know that he'd been waiting his entire life for Bree, but now that he had her in his arms, and in his bed, there was no way he was going to walk away from her. Not because she wasn't ready to mate.

It would come.

Of that he was confident.

He had to be.

"Okay," he said after a moment.

"Okay?"

She looked so sexy, sitting there in front of him with her hair hanging over her breasts, just tickling her nipples. Liam had to fight the urge to push her back down against the mattress and show her exactly how okay it would be.

"Yes," he said, settling instead for a hand on her thigh. "It's okay. I get it. Everything has been really fast. I'm not in a hurry."

"You're not?"

Liam chuckled. "Of course not. I have you now. You're mine and I'm yours, and as long as I have that, I can wait on everything else. Including making you my mate."

Her smile was enough to steel his resolve. It was the right decision.

For now.

Chapter Thirteen

LIAM COULDN'T REMEMBER the last time he'd enjoyed himself as much as he had the last few days. Being with Bree was like seeing everything through fresh eyes.

She'd taken to her bear so well. Better than even he could have imagined. But she was still worried about what it would mean now that she'd recognized her animal. *Would her clan find her? Would they hunt her down?*

Liam could tell she was trying not to let it bother her, but he could see through it. It was weighing on her. And because it was troubling her, it was troubling him. He'd woken up that morning determined to find her some answers.

There was only one way to know whether Bree's concerns were unfounded or not. And that involved a visit to Jackson Valley to talk to some of the elders who knew more than he did. And he wasn't the only one who knew it. He'd snuck down to the kitchen to get Bree a cup of coffee when his brother, sister, and cousins found him.

"We need to talk." Ryker leaned against the counter and crossed his arms. "It's about Bree."

Liam stiffened and set the mug he was holding down. "What about Bree?"

"More like Bree's family," Luke said. "If she's scared, there's a reason."

Liam nodded. He couldn't agree more.

"Where are they from?"

"Colorado." It was all Liam knew. "Bree was never told what town they fled from. All she knows is that they were in Colorado. At least, she's pretty sure of it." The details were very thin, given that Bree was so young when everything happened and her guardians had been pretty thin on the details.

"We need to find out who they are," Axel said. "If Bree's story is true, we—"

"Of course it's true!" Liam pulled his shoulders back and glared at his cousin. "She wouldn't lie about something like that."

"Stand down, cousin." Luke put a hand on Liam's chest and stepped between them. "That's not what Axel is saying."

"Then what exactly is he saying?" Liam shook Luke's hand off, but he didn't step back.

"I'm saying that Bree was very young when all this happened and all she has to go on is what her grandparents or I guess, in reality, her *guardians* told her. Who knows what the truth really is. But no matter what, if the Sterling clan was willing to kill because of a mated match, there's a good chance that Bree's right and they'd be willing to kill to get rid of the evidence of that match."

It was a reality that Liam had considered since he heard Bree's story, but hearing it from someone else made his blood run cold. He wouldn't let anything happen to his mate. Not ever. He shook his head. "I won't let them get near her."

Next to him, his sister chuckled and shook her head. "I

appreciate that, brother, but you can't be with her all of the time. And it's not just Bree we need to be worried about."

He spun to stare at Natalia. "What do you mean?"

"What she means," Axel said, "is that if there's a clan out there that's willing to hunt Bree down and kill her, that puts everyone at risk."

"All of us," Ryker added.

"And our mates." Luke crossed his arms over his chest and nodded.

Liam looked in turn at each member of his family and finally locked eyes with Axel. "What are you saying?" The hairs on the back of his neck stood at attention and his hands curled into fists at his side. Family or not, if they were implying that Bree wasn't welcome with them at Grizzly Ridge, it would come to blows, of that much he was sure.

"Seriously, Liam." Natalia put her hands on his shoulders. He stiffened, but then she squeezed and said, "We're here to help." He turned to look at her. There was nothing but sincerity in her eyes. "We love Bree," she said. "And we love you. Whatever is going on, we're going to find out."

"We need to stay ahead of it," Axel said. "For the sake of our families."

"And that includes Bree," Luke added. "Of course it includes Bree."

"I agree." Satisfied, Liam released a breath and relaxed his posture. "I was going to take a trip back to the valley and see if there was anyone there who might know something about the Sterling clan. The elders there might remember something."

Natalia nodded. "It's a good idea. But I can go."

"No." Liam shook his head. "I know you're trying to keep me away from Jackson Valley right now, but I need to do this. Besides, I'm good with your decision about the clan." It wasn't a lie. It wasn't too long ago that he wasn't okay with her decision at all to rule the clan with a committee, mostly because he felt as though he was the man for the job. But things had changed. He had clarity now where he didn't have it before.

Thanks to your mate.

Whatever it was and wherever it had come from, it didn't matter. He wasn't lying to Natalia when he'd said he was good with it. He was. "I need to do this, Nat. I need to go."

She looked as if she might protest again, but then she nodded. "Okay. Ryker and I will stay here." Ryker gave her a look. He wasn't used to being bossed around by his little sister, but then he nodded and crossed his arms over his chest. "Axel? Luke?"

"No." The brothers each shook their heads. "We'll stay here."

Liam narrowed his eyes in question. He would have thought that Axel and Luke both would have jumped at the chance of going to see Tonia. After all, they hadn't seen their mother since they were small children. And now that everything had changed within the clan, and there was no more exile, it was a chance for a new start. Or at least a fresh one. "I don't mind going by myself, but don't you want to—"

"No." Axel looked him straight in the eyes, shutting down any further questions. "We have no plans to stir up drama and cause any more stress around here than there already is. Not right now."

"I respect that." Natalia nodded.

But Ryker shook his head. "She's your mother. You should—"

"I appreciate that you think you know what we should do." It was Luke who interrupted him. "But to say it's a delicate situation would be putting it mildly. There's no way Kira could deal with her mother who abandoned her as a child with the stress of being a new mom. Never mind the fact that Kade is wound so tight right now waiting for the birth of his own child that bringing her into it would set him off completely."

Axel nodded. "We'll wait."

"We've waited this long. Another few weeks won't make any difference."

There was no point in arguing with them. Besides, Liam had bigger, more pressing concerns. "Okay, then I'll go alone."

FOR TWO DAYS, Bree and Liam lived in a winter fantasy land at Grizzly Ridge. Bree had managed to get a hold of the part-time worker she'd had helping her out at the store from time to time and convinced her to work a few extra hours, so she didn't have to go back into town to open Bree's Knees and could instead spend her time with Liam and the others.

As much as she loved her store, she was enjoying her time at the ridge far too much to leave. And it wasn't just the ridge.

It was her bear.

After that first run where she'd shifted, they'd gone twice more. Each time it got a little bit easier and she was able to last longer. Bree was positive she would never get used to the feeling of letting her animal take over so completely. It was almost like trusting a stranger with your life.

But it wasn't a stranger.

It was her bear.

And more and more, Bree was learning that as much as she tried to hide it for so long, her bear really was an integral part of who she was. Never in her whole life had she felt so *alive*. Colors were brighter, sounds were sweeter, sex was better.

Although, she was pretty sure she could give all of that credit to Liam and the crazy connection they shared.

To say that it was hot would be a complete understatement. When they came together—which was as often as possible—it was combustible. She'd never had a lot of experience with men before, but the little she did have didn't come close to what she shared with Liam. It was like a romance novel come to life, a fantasy she never wanted to wake up from. *And that was fine by her because when he touched—*

"I feel like I'm interrupting something." Harper's voice interrupted her thoughts only seconds before they could get really dirty.

"You did." Bree laughed, but didn't bother denying it. "But it's nothing I can't get back to later." She extended her arms for Harper's baby girl, Lily. "But I'm happy to see you." She wiggled her nose against Lily's, making the baby laugh.

"Happy to see me?" Harper teased. "Or the baby?"

"Both, of course." She nodded with her head. "Sit. Let's catch up. I feel like the last few days have been a total blur."

Harper sat cross-legged on the couch next to her and grabbed a throw blanket for her lap. "I'm sure it has." She shook her head. "I still can't believe all this, Bree. I mean, I can't believe we didn't know. How did we not know?"

Bree focused on the baby to keep from looking her friend in the eye. Now that the Jacksons all knew her secret and were so welcoming, without any hesitation, the guilt for lying to them had started to hit her.

"I'm really sorry, Harper. I wanted to tell you." That was a lie. She shook her head and tried again. "That's not true," she said honestly this time. "I didn't actually want to tell you." She took a breath and looked up at her friend. "I didn't even want to acknowledge it myself. I wanted to ignore it all. And the craziest part is, I thought I could."

"Well, you kind of did." Harper's smile was kind. "For a long time you ignored it. And really, I'm very impressed."

"Why? You ignored your bear side." After Harper met Axel, it was discovered that she was actually half shifter. Something she had no idea about.

"That was different. I didn't know about it. You knew the whole time who you were, and fought it every day."

Bree hadn't really thought about it that way before. But now that she'd embraced her true self, there was a lightness about her that had never been there before. It was crazy to think that she'd been living her life under a constant state of stress for so long.

Never again.

"Where is Liam, anyway? I've barely seen the two of you apart."

Bree laughed. They really had been inseparable up until a few hours ago. "He said he was going up to Jackson Valley for a few hours."

Jackson Valley was only a short drive away, but up until a few months ago it might as well have been a world away as far as most of the Jacksons were concerned. Axel, Luke, and Kade had been exiled when Kira ran off with a man she felt at the time was her fated mate—he wasn't. It had taken a few years for them all to come back to one another, but now the family bonds were once again mended. And with the recent death of Gordon Jackson, the patriarch of the clan, things had changed once again. Now the Jackson clan was run by three alphas: Natalia, Luke, and Natalia's mother, Kristine. Bree didn't know much about the way clans were run, but with Axel the alpha of Grizzly Ridge and a group running the rest of the Jackson clan, things seemed a lot more peaceful and fair than what she knew about the Sterling clan that had been her family.

"I actually thought that Axel would go along to talk to—"

Bree bit her lip, already afraid she'd said too much. Liam had told her that Tonia—Axel, Luke, Kade, and Kira's mother—had returned after many years of being gone from the clan, but Bree wasn't sure who knew. She did know for sure that Kira definitely didn't know her mother was back. They'd wanted to wait to tell her until after the babies were born and she was settled back at home so they didn't upset her.

Bree had never met the woman, and she wasn't about to

presume that she knew her story. But she felt for her, none-theless. It couldn't be easy to walk away from your children, no matter what the circumstances were.

"I know Tonia is back," Harper said matter-of-factly. "It's okay, Bree. I know. Axel told me. I wish he would have gone today as well." She picked up a throw pillow and squeezed it tight to her chest. "He's been so quiet about it all, I don't even really know how he's dealing with it. He won't talk to me about it. All he'll say is that it's not the right time."

Bree nodded. "I can't imagine there'll ever be a *right time.*"

"Right? But maybe he's right and it's better to wait until after Kira is settled in with the babies. It will be hardest on Kira. I may be partial, but I think there's something very special about a mother and daughter's relationship."

Bree ignored the twinge of pain in her chest. She barely even remembered her mother, but certainly they would have been close if she'd lived. She focused on the baby on her lap. She was so sweet. So innocent. Her heart clenched the way it always did when she held baby Lily. "She has her entire life ahead of her." She wasn't speaking to anyone specifically, but next to her, she noticed Harper nod at the change of topic.

"Maybe one day—"

They were interrupted by the front door opening and the arrival of Kira, Nash, and the twins.

"You're here!" Harper jumped up and ran to the door to help Nash with the two car seats. "Oh my goodness. I think they're even cuter than the last time I saw them."

Kira smiled. "They're cute, all right. But I don't think I'll ever sleep again."

Bree snuggled Lily close to her chest and got up to greet the new family. "I'm so glad you're home."

Kira walked straight over to Bree and pulled her in for a hug, the baby between them. "I'm so glad that *you* are home."

Bree nodded and blinked back the tears that suddenly

threatened. They both knew what Kira meant. It was just about the most perfect thing she could have said.

"So," Bree changed topics. "Are you going to tell us their names yet, or what?"

Nash chuckled and shook his head. They'd moved into the great room and put the car seat carriers with the sleeping infants on the floor close enough to the fireplace that they would stay nice and warm. "We would tell you," he said. "If we knew ourselves."

"You still don't know?"

Nash wrapped an arm around his mate and grinned. "She can't decide on the girl's name. So I've been sworn to secrecy on the boy name."

"Hey," Kira said. "It's a huge decision. They'll have these names their entire lives."

"That's how it works." Bree laughed. "I'm sure whatever you choose will be perfect."

"Choose?" Zoe and Ella came in from the kitchen, carrying a tray of peppermint hot chocolate. "You still haven't chosen names?" Zoe shook her head as she put the tray of drinks down.

Ella followed behind at a much slower pace. She had grown even larger in the last few days, something Bree wasn't even sure was possible, and she'd started to waddle as she walked.

"Ella? Are you feeling okay?"

"I'm feeling like this baby can come any day now, *mi amiga*." She smiled, but it didn't quite reach her eyes as she fell backward into the couch. "Kira, I'm very jealous of you right now. What I wouldn't give for this little one to come out and say hi."

"Soon, my friend." Kira sat next to her and handed her a mug to sip on. "What a fun holiday it would be if all the babies were here."

"I can't think of a better present."

In her arms, Lily started to fuss and automatically Bree bounced the baby, but she wanted her mama. Reluctantly, Bree handed her back and as soon as she did, her arms felt oddly empty. She'd never given much thought to having children of her own. Not really. But now with Liam and…could it be that things had changed *that* much in such a short time?

Yes. It's definitely possible.

"THE STERLING CLAN…" The elder bear nodded and scratched his chin. "Sterling…" The man rocked in his chair and gazed out the window past where Liam paced. He'd tried being patient with the old man, but he was quickly getting to the end of his rope with him. "From Colorado, you say…"

"Harry." Liam spun and stared at the man. "Do you know them—"

"Liam." Kristine, his mother, raised a cautionary hand.

He knew she was worried about his temper but he had it under control. At least he thought he had. That was before Bree. Every single one of his emotions were amped up since Bree came into his life. It was almost as if his bear had a frenetic energy about him. An energy Liam had no idea how to harness.

"Relax," Kristine said. "Harry is just thinking out loud. I'm sure if he knows something, he'll tell you."

"Oh, I know the Sterling clan."

Both of them turned to stare at the old man.

"You do?" Liam stepped closer. "Why didn't you just say that?"

Kristine shook her head. It had been her idea to talk to Harry, but Liam could see that even she was growing weary with the conversation. "What do you know?" she rephrased. "Are they dangerous?"

"Dangerous?" Harry looked confused for a moment before he looked directly at Liam. "Aren't all grizzlies dangerous?"

Liam shook his head and tried again. "What my mom means is, would they kill one of their own?"

Again, the old man looked confused.

Liam sighed. "This is ridiculous. We're not getting anywhere." He turned back to the window and looked out onto the snowy yard. Behind him, he could hear his mom move closer to Harry.

"Tell us what you know, Harry." She spoke softly—a direct contrast to Liam's agitation. Of course, it wasn't *her* mate at risk. "It's important. We have reason to believe that the Sterling clan might be dangerous to one of our own and we want to make sure that if there is a risk, she's safe."

"I don't know much." Harry's voice was shaky. "But I remember hearing a story years ago. A legend more than anything, about a mated pair who was killed."

Liam turned and listened.

"Go on," Kristine urged. "Did they hunt them and kill them? Was it because the clan didn't approve of their chosen mate? Why would they do that?"

Harry rubbed his chin between two fingers. "There was a story," he said after a moment. "But time has a way of changing things."

"What was it?" As much as he'd tried, Liam couldn't hold back.

"The girl, the Sterling, she chose a mate from the King clan."

"King?"

Harry nodded. "The King clan is found mostly in Northern Canada, and they have a reputation for being a little rough around the edges."

"That's saying something." Kristine chuckled a little under her breath.

"It is," Harry continued. "And the Sterling clan wasn't super happy about it. You see, Sterlings have long had a reputation for being a little more highbrow than others. Always a little more important. A little better than the others. They didn't want anything to do with back country Kings. Especially if a union resulted in cubs. But the couple, they didn't care. They were going to be together."

"So her clan members hunted them and killed them? They were unhappy enough to do that?"

Harry nodded. "That was one story."

Liam's stomach churned. "How could they hate her choice so much that they'd kill one of their own?" He shook his head. "It doesn't make sense. We don't...bears don't..."

"Like I said," Harry interrupted. "Time has a way of changing things. And that was only one story."

"What do you mean by that?" The old man looked to Kristine, who'd asked the question. "Do you believe that's how it happened? That the Sterlings could really hate so much that they'd kill their own?"

Harry shrugged. "Remember, that was second-hand information. And there were a few stories. I can't be sure which one is true. It was a long time ago."

There was more to it; Liam *knew* it. He could feel it. The old man knew something more that he wasn't saying. But he yawned and closed his eyes, and Liam knew that he wasn't going to get much more out of the old man than he already had.

"Thank you, Harry."

He nodded but didn't open his eyes.

"If you remember anything else," Liam added. "Anything at all...please let us know."

He waited, but Harry didn't say anything else, so they

turned to leave. Liam opened the front door and a blast of winter air hit him in the face, so he almost missed it when behind him Harry spoke up again.

"What did you say?" Liam turned, putting his back to the door.

"Tonia," Harry repeated. "She might know more."

"Tonia?" Kristine looked to Liam. "You mean my sister, Tonia? How would she know anything?"

Harry opened his eyes. "She was mated to a Sterling."

Chapter Fourteen

ONLY TWO DAYS BEFORE CHRISTMAS, Grizzly Ridge was a hive of activity and Bree was completely satisfied to be wrapped up in all of the festive fun. Besides the baking, present wrapping, and final preparations, there were two newborn babies to cuddle and a very cranky, teething baby Lily who wouldn't let her poor mother put her down for more than ten minutes at a time.

"Are you sure you don't mind, Bree?" Harper asked for the dozenth time in the last few minutes as she paced the floor with baby Lily, who, for the moment, was satisfied to suck on a cold teething ring. "I mean, it's so last minute and—"

"I told you," Bree interrupted with a smile. "I'm happy to do it. I only wished I had thought of it earlier."

Watching Harper earlier that morning trying to juggle the baby while stirring up dough for a fresh batch of cookies, Bree was struck with inspiration that had her pulling her sewing machine out.

If the baby wouldn't let her mother put her down long enough for Harper to get anything done, Bree could fix that by sewing up a baby-wearing sling for Harper.

"It's actually going to be pretty easy," Bree said. "I'm just glad I thought to grab my sewing machine when Liam took me down into town yesterday." He hadn't wanted her to go back to town at all, claiming it would be safer for her at the ridge until they knew more about her family, but Bree had insisted. She loved it at Grizzly Ridge, but she still had a shop to worry about down in town. Besides, she'd wanted to find a little something for a Christmas present for Liam. Not that she'd been all that successful on that front. Not with him standing guard everywhere she went. But she did have one idea that she hoped he would like.

In the meantime, she had to whip up the sling to give Harper some relief from her demanding baby. "I'm so glad this tablecloth is big enough." Harper laughed and shook her head at the huge piece of fabric decorated with wreaths and candy canes that she'd found in a back cupboard. "I guess if we open the doors to guests next Christmas, I'll have to replace it. But it'll be worth it, if it works."

"It will." Bree nodded and got back to work cutting the fabric into a long strip. "It'll only be a few minutes."

She turned back to her sewing.

"Do you think this was all a mistake?" Harper said after a moment.

"A mistake?" Bree lifted her head briefly. "What exactly are you talking about?"

"This." Harper sounded close to tears. "Christmas. The Reindeer Games. A big dinner. Just...all of it." Her friend's voice shook.

Bree finished pinning the two pieces of fabric together and watched Harper as she stopped pacing in front of the Christmas tree.

She looked up and took it all in before turning back to Bree. "I think it might have been a mistake."

"No." Bree shook her head and offered Harper a small smile. "It wasn't a mistake."

"I just wanted so badly to make it all perfect, you know?"

Bree didn't but she nodded, nonetheless.

"My whole life, I wanted a big family Christmas and now that I have Lily...well, I just thought that I could give her everything that the holiday is supposed to be."

Bree pushed back her chair and stood. "You are giving her everything. But you know that Christmas doesn't have to be a huge production for it to be good, right? It's not about the decorations and the games and the food."

"It is." Harper spun. "Have you never seen a Hallmark movie?"

Bree couldn't help but laugh out loud. "Right, but we don't live in a Hallmark movie."

"That's probably a good thing," Harper agreed.

"It is." She put an arm on her friend's shoulder and squeezed. "All you need to give Lily is love. That's it. And she has that in abundance with this family."

Harper wiped a tear from her cheek.

"Don't be so hard on yourself. Never mind that you're a new mother. There is so much going on around here, I can't believe you took on even more."

"I am kind of crazy."

"The best kind."

Harper laughed. "Thank you for being such a good friend."

"You know I'm going to say the same thing right back to you. I don't know what I would have done if you all hadn't been so welcoming of me now that the truth is out."

"I still can't believe you hid it for so long." Harper wiped at her face and gave the baby a quick kiss on her forehead. "Are you any closer to learning anything about your clan?"

Bree shook her head.

Liam had returned from his trip to Jackson Valley but hadn't told her much about his visit. "He said that no one really knew anything." She shrugged and returned to her sewing machine, determined to get the project finished for Harper. "But I didn't really expect him to learn anything. Besides, I don't feel any different and you'd think that if they really could sense me and track me, they would have already. Right?"

Harper shrugged. "I don't know enough about all of this, to be honest. But I'm sure you're perfectly safe here with us. No one is going to let anything happen to you."

Bree smiled. Of that she was sure.

"Especially with Liam as your mate," Harper continued. "He's a strong bear. He would never...what?"

Bree had blushed and looked away. She'd hoped Harper wouldn't notice, but her friend was too astute. "I haven't...we haven't..."

"You haven't mated?" Harper's mouth fell open. "I thought for sure that once you shifted and...no? Really?"

"Really." She ran the fabric through the machine to keep from looking at her friend. The truth was that although she'd told Liam she wanted to wait for a little bit so she could process everything that was happening, that was only part of the truth.

She was terrified.

Right now everything was perfect with Liam. She was happy. He was happy. What was the point to change anything? Besides, what would change? They'd already said they were committed to each other. She couldn't possibly need the mark to prove it. *Right?*

"Why not?" Harper had come to stand directly in front of her at the table. "What are you waiting for?"

She shrugged. "I just don't think it's a big deal. I mean, what would—"

"You don't think it's a big deal?" Dumbfounded, her friend

shook her head and took a step backward. "You don't even… you're missing out, girl. Mating…well, it's next level."

Bree laughed. "Things are pretty next level right now."

"You have no idea."

She shook her head. It was too much to think of right now. One thing at a time. She finished sewing the final seam and pulled the material from the machine before snipping the threads. "Come try this. I think I know how they work."

Glad for the distraction, it took a few minutes, but before long Bree managed to wrap baby Lily into the length of fabric and tie it securely around Harper so that the baby was perched up high on her mother's back. "There." She clapped her hands and took a step back. "It looks awesome."

Harper moved across the room to the full-length mirror by the front door. "Oh my God. It looks fantastic, Bree. Thank you! And she looks so happy. This is fantastic."

"I'm so glad it worked." Satisfied, Bree went to tuck her sewing machine away.

"Me too." Harper bounced up and down a bit. "And now we can finish up the Reindeer Games the way I'd planned. If Lily is happy, I can finally get things done. I'm going to go get Axel and set up for the snowshoe races. Tell the others."

As Harper bounced out of the room, the only thing Bree could do was laugh. So much for relaxing, and not needing a big Christmas.

"THIS IS CRAZY." Liam shook his head and bent to fasten his snowshoes. "I thought Harper was exhausted and with the new babies and…why are we doing this again?"

Bree shrugged. "It's important to Harper." She smiled and Liam's groin tightened. *How was it that even wearing a puffy parka, she was still the sexiest woman he'd ever seen?*

And more so, that even standing in the freezing temperatures, his body was on fire for her?

He liked it.

A lot.

"And it's going to be fun to kick your ass?" She laughed as he straightened up.

"You think so, do you?"

"Oh, I know so." She laughed again. "You haven't seen all my moves yet. I am a pro snowshoer."

"Is that right?"

She nodded and turned so quickly Liam almost tripped on his own snowshoes.

"I'll race you to the start line."

Liam laughed. "We're on the same team!" Nevertheless, he turned and ran after her.

He was taller and stronger than her, but Bree was surprisingly agile with the clunky snowshoes strapped to her feet. Plus she had a head start. Even so, Liam caught up to her and wrapped his arms around her waist.

He tripped and started going down, taking her with him. Fortunately, he was quick and able to turn so he landed in the deep snow and she landed on top of him. With his arms wrapped tight around her, she was pinned safely to his chest.

"Caught you."

"I let you catch me." She winked. "Because then I could do this." She pressed a kiss on his lips and Liam tightened his grip. She groaned into it as his tongue found hers.

The race be dammed, he'd quite happily spend the rest of the day right there.

Or in a soft bed.

Or up against a—

"Get a room, you two!"

Bree pulled away and laughed. Liam looked over her shoulder, up at Cyrus, who loomed over them with a smile on his face.

"I was just thinking of doing exactly that," he said to his friend.

Bree pushed up and off him, and a moment later, Liam got to his feet as well.

"No deal," Cyrus said. "It's race time. And if I'm racing, you're racing. No way I'm going to pass up an opportunity to kick my brother-in-law's ass."

"Can you even say that if you're not married?" Bree wrapped her arm around his waist.

"Sure can," Cyrus said. "Bears don't marry."

"Except for Harper." Natalia joined them. "But then again, Harper does a lot of human things."

"Like Reindeer Games?"

"I don't know if those can be considered human." She used her fingers to make air quotes. "You'd know better, Bree."

Next to him, Bree blushed and shook her head. It seemed so natural just to think of Bree as a grizzly shifter, that he still sometimes forgot that she was raised as a human. "I guess I don't think of it that way," she said. "All of this…" She waved her free arm in a circle. "It's just a *thing*. Not shifter. Not human. Just whatever makes you happy. And this big Christmas celebration is making Harper happy."

"Yes, it is." Axel arrived at the starting line with a whistle and a clipboard in his hand. "And if my mate is happy, I'm happy. So all of you need to line up and get ready to race."

There were a few chuckles, some mumbling and grumbling, and even a hoot as the group gathered on the start line. Harper, wearing her new baby sling over her parka, explained the rules. Kira and Nash, of course, were in their cabin, staying warm with the babies but Ella and Kade were there. Although they weren't racing, Ella didn't want to miss any part of her first North American Christmas.

More and more lately, as Liam looked at the women at the ridge with their new babies and pregnant bellies, he couldn't help but imagine Bree carrying his child one day soon.

Did she even want children?

They hadn't even discussed it. He glanced in her direction. She was smiling and nodding as Harper went over the directions for the game. Liam was only half listening, but it involved finding ornaments and being the first to cross the finish line as a team.

Bree grew up as an only child in the worst situation. *Maybe she wouldn't want to bring children into a world that could be so unfair and scary?* It was just one of many thoughts that had popped into Liam's head over the last few days.

Especially after leaving Jackson Valley with the truth. The truth he still hadn't told Bree.

After he'd left Harry, he'd gone directly in search of his Aunt Tonia.

He'd found her in the kitchen of the main house, drinking coffee, and she didn't look surprised to see him.

"LIAM." Tonia had greeted him with a tight hug. "I'm glad you're here. Natalia said you were going to lay low for a little bit."

"I am." He kissed her on the cheek. "But I had some important business here today. And…" He pulled back to look at his aunt. "I was hoping to meet with you as well."

He'd only met her briefly before leaving for Grizzly Ridge, and, to be honest, hadn't paid much attention. But it was easy to see which side of the family Kira took after. She looked exactly like her mother, with the same long, dark hair and green eyes.

"Well, I'm sure happy to see you." Tonia pulled out of his

embrace and gestured to the table. "I've been looking forward to getting to know all of you and of course seeing my own…" She drifted off and her eyes took on a faraway look before refocusing on him. "Anyway, it's been nice to find out about Kristine and all of you."

Liam was taken aback. He hadn't considered that Tonia wouldn't have known about his mother or any of them. But of course, she'd been long gone before Kristine had sought out the Jackson clan. It wasn't until her own mate had died—the rest of her family already gone—that she went looking for her birth father, Gordon Jackson. Kristine and her children had been a surprise to everyone.

"That must be…well…" He didn't know what would be appropriate to say, so he just nodded his head and moved across the room to pour himself a cup of coffee.

It wasn't until they were all sitting at the table that he said what he'd come to find out. "I know we don't know each other very well," he started cautiously, trying for some tact. It wasn't his strong suit. "And I know there's a lot of…well…" He looked to his mother for help, but she only smiled. "There's a lot of emotions, I'm sure, with you coming back to the Jackson clan."

"There are." Her smile was soft and sad. He could imagine that if she was happy, she would look just like Kira.

Kira, who, as far as Liam knew, still didn't know that her mother had returned.

He swallowed hard.

"I took a chance," Tonia said. "And my father actually surprised me. We were able to make peace before he passed. It was…" She looked down at the table for a moment before once more meeting his eyes. "But it wasn't my father I came back for."

"Your children."

She nodded. "I haven't quite worked up the courage to reach out." A tear slipped from her cheek. "They must…well, I guess I don't know how they must feel. I so badly want them to understand, to—"

"They know," Liam interrupted. He didn't know Tonia. Only what he'd been told. That she'd made a choice many years ago. Maybe it was an impossible choice. He used to think it couldn't possibly be that hard. After all, how could one choose anyone at all over their own children? Especially a mother? But now that he had Bree, his fated mate, his previous hard stance had softened a little. Maybe it hadn't been so cut and dry after all. "Well," he continued. "They don't *all* know." He shook his head. "Kira doesn't know yet."

Tonia's tears fell openly and Liam felt his heart clench for her. It didn't take much to see that the woman clearly ached for her children.

"I need to see them."

"I'm sure you do, Tonia. But—"

"You don't understand, Kristine. I need to see them. I can't wait another day."

"You'll have to." Liam spoke calmly, but Tonia whipped her head around to stare at him. "I'm sure you know but Kira just gave birth to twins."

The woman clutched at her chest and nodded.

"I knew. I could feel it."

"They were born early. It wasn't an easy pregnancy."

Tonia's lips curled up. "Shifter twins never are," she said wistfully. "I should have been there for her."

"She's fine," Liam continued. "But they need to settle in. Axel and Luke don't want to tell her until after things have calmed down."

"And Kade?" The woman's eyes challenged him. Her children had been so young when she'd left them, but she obviously knew their dynamics. "What does Kade want?"

Kade was and had always been the wild card, but in this he was crystal-clear. "Kade's mate is due to give birth herself any day," Liam said. "Kade isn't interested in adding more stress to Grizzly Ridge right now than there already is." It was a tactful way to say that Kade had flat out refused to see their mother. But just as he'd been with their grandfather before he passed, everyone was certain he'd come around and change his mind.

They sat in silence for a moment while that sank in. Finally, Liam brought up the subject he'd been hoping to find answers for. "I need your help, Tonia. I was just in to see Harry. He's one of the most elder grizzlies we have," Liam explained, "and I need some information on something that happened a long time ago. I was hoping he'd remember and be able to help me out."

"And did he?"

Liam nodded. "He did." He looked at his aunt. "I was looking for information about the Sterling clan." Her face changed at the mention of the name. "He said you were mated to a Sterling. Is that true?"

She didn't answer at first, but then finally nodded. "I was. We were fated and he was the love of my life."

"That's who you left your children for?"

"It wasn't that simple," she shot back. "But that's an explanation for them."

Liam could respect that. His cousins deserved to hear directly from their mother what had happened all those years ago. "Okay. But the Sterlings? I need to know if you remember a situation that happened about twenty years ago."

Tonia looked into her mug and didn't respond for so long that Liam began to wonder whether she'd heard him at all. Finally, she looked up. "A situation?"

He nodded.

"A couple ended up dead," she said slowly. "Their child went missing. Is that what you mean?"

His heart sped up and his foot bounced a rapid beat on the floor beneath the table. "That's it! What do you know?"

"I know everything. And I'll tell you," she said slowly. "But I need something from you."

BREE LISTENED ATTENTIVELY to Harper's instructions.

Check the map, stay in the flagged-off area, and find four red ball ornaments hiding in the trees. First couple back to the start line, wins.

Easy.

"If there aren't any questions, let's get started." Harper looked to Axel, who handed her the whistle. "Competitors, get ready," she called out and someone groaned.

Bree laughed and glanced at Liam, a competitive smile fixed to her face. She was so ready to win this.

"On your marks!"

The smile fell from Bree's face when Liam wouldn't meet her eyes. He was looking into the trees, a faraway expression on his face, as if he were anywhere but there with her.

"Liam?" She elbowed him in the side. "Are you ready?"

"Get set!" Harper hollered, obviously enjoying herself.

"Liam?"

He blinked hard and glanced at her, once more focused on where he was.

"Go!"

Bree looked at Harper as she blew the whistle and then back to Liam.

"Let's go." He grabbed her gloved hand in his.

She made a note to ask him about what he was thinking about later. But it would have to wait because they had a race to win. "Let's go!"

Together, they started running in their snowshoes through the deep snow. They'd only gone a few steps before Liam tripped over his own feet.

"I'm going down!"

Bree yanked on his hand and somehow kept him upright. "Not today, mister."

They laughed and slowed their pace as competitors all around them crashed to the ground in puffs of snow.

Bree looked ahead and could see Zoe and Gabe, clearly seasoned snowshoers, disappear into the trees to the left. "Let's go right," she said to Liam. He seemed pleased to let her take charge, and with the competition fueling her, she dragged him along behind her.

Once they got into the trees, they slowed their pace considerably as they scanned the trees for the ornaments. Harper had said they would be at eye level so there was no need to search too hard for them. But with the thick trees and the branches covered in snow, it was proving challenging to find their first one.

But then, there it was. "There!" Liam pointed through the trees, his voice full of excitement like a little boy on Christmas morning, and Bree couldn't help but laugh.

"What's so funny?"

"I just think you're cute." She kissed him on the cheek, the competition momentarily forgotten.

"Well, I think you're pretty damn cute yourself." He took her face in his gloved hands and kissed her thoroughly. "But I still think you want to win."

Bree laughed again and finally looked to where he pointed. The sun shone off the red glass and once she saw it, she couldn't believe she hadn't seen it earlier. It was so obvious.

But all things were, once you found them.

"Go grab it, babe."

Carefully, Bree picked her way across the snow, through the trees, and plucked the ornament off the branch. It had a clip on the end, so Bree fastened it to her coat and rejoined Liam.

"Only three more to go. Let's get moving. I think Zoe and Gabe will be the ones to beat."

"Well then, let's beat them."

IT TOOK them another twenty minutes, but Liam and Bree managed to find another three ornaments. Watching Bree and how much she got into the competition was a total turn-on for Liam—although everything when it came to Bree was a turn-on for Liam.

"Let's get back," he said once she had the fourth one clipped to her coat. "Too bad we can't shift. I could get there *way* faster."

Bree laughed. "It's against the rules and there's no way I'm getting disqualified because you can't run fast in those things."

Liam pretended to look offended. He pressed a hand to his chest. "Hey, I'm getting better."

"Well then, let's go."

She took off running and for a second, he was so busy enjoying the view he forgot he was supposed to be going with her. But only for a second. He wasn't going to let her down. Not when it came to a silly snowshoe race, and not when it came to finding out more about her family. Not when it came to *anything*. He was *never* going to let his mate down.

His bear growled as he moved. Liam knew his bear was getting restless about taking Bree as his mate. He also knew that he'd have a much easier time convincing her when she knew the truth about her family. He knew he'd always keep her safe. But he needed her to know it and more importantly, really believe it.

"Come on, Liam!"

He was falling a bit behind, so he picked up the pace, concentrating on each footstep. They broke out of the trees and there it was. The finish line.

Also, there was Gabe and Zoe.

And Nina and Ryker?

They'd been some of the early ones to crash into the snow. No way they'd caught up to them.

With a fresh burst of energy, Liam grabbed Bree's hand and together they picked up speed.

Neck and neck with Zoe and Gabe, Liam could feel Ryker and Nina closing in on them.

"Come on!" Bree hollered.

His first instinct was to laugh at how competitive she'd become, but he didn't because he'd become equally competitive. Fueled by the need to win, Liam tapped into his bear and with Bree's hand still in his, propelled them across the finish line, where they collapsed into the snow.

Right next to Zoe and Gabe.

Liam looked over at his friend lying next to him and locked eyes with Gabe. They both laughed and shook their heads. A moment later, Ryker and Natalia crashed to the ground as well in a cloud of snow that drifted over them all.

"Did we win?" Bree sat up next to him and looked around. "Did we beat them?"

Harper and Axel appeared with the clipboard, both of them shaking their heads and laughing. "I had no idea our friends and family were so cutthroat," Axel said to his mate. "Did you?"

"No clue."

"Did we win?" Bree asked again.

"We won," Zoe piped up good-naturedly.

"No way—it was us." Ryker laughed, knowing full well that they most definitely had *not* won, and Liam threw snow at his brother.

"I think it's a tie." Harper looked between them. "Our first ever tie."

"To be fair," Liam said, "it's the first ever Reindeer Games.

But I'll take a tie." He extended a hand to Gabe. "Good work, guys."

Instead of taking his hand, Gabe threw a handful of snow at him. As the icy wetness melted and ran down Liam's face, he laughed and grabbed up another armful of snow.

And then it was on. Snow flew everywhere. Laughs and screeches filled the air as more and more of the Jackson clan crossed the finish line and joined in.

Finally, exhausted, cold, and soaked, the snow fight was over and Harper blew her whistle, laughing as she did so. "Let's get inside."

Liam groaned and pulled Bree into his arms. He kissed her wet nose before kissing her properly. The only event he wanted to participate in was going to involve the two of them, alone, in bed.

Chapter Fifteen

"I CAN'T REMEMBER the last time I laughed so hard." Bree pulled off her wet sweater and dropped it on the floor before turning to tug her leggings off. She was soaked to the bone, despite her parka and snow pants. But it didn't matter; the race had been more fun than even she had expected and judging by the look on Liam's face, he'd had a good time as well.

She turned to face him, wearing nothing but her bra and panties, and the look on his face was an entirely different one.

One she liked. A lot.

"I can think of another way to have a little fun." He took a step toward her and instantly heat pooled in her panties.

The ability this man had to turn her on was ridiculous. And amazing. And like nothing she'd ever experienced. But one thing was sure: she couldn't get enough.

"Is that right?" She lowered her eyes and licked her bottom lip.

Never in her life had she behaved in such a way with a man.

Of course, never in her life had she *had* such a man.

Maybe she should just give in and mate with him? What was the problem anyway? Why was she holding back on that?

"Hey." Liam stepped up and rubbed his thumb against her cheek. "Did I lose you there for a second?"

He was so in tune with her already. So connected.

Imagine what it will be like when you're mated.

She shook her head in an effort to clear it. "Sorry, I was just…it doesn't matter." Bree stood on her tiptoes, wrapped her arms around his neck, and kissed him deep enough that it really didn't matter at all. Because the only thing that did matter was the two of them. Right there, wanting each other.

And Liam *did* want her. She could feel how much he wanted her. Not only in her heart, but also physically, with his thick, hard rod pressed up against her stomach. Just knowing how badly he wanted her turned Bree on even more.

She wiggled against him, pressing her body up as close as she possibly could.

"Damn, woman. Do you have any idea what you do to me?"

She grinned. "Oh, I have a pretty good idea."

Just as she knew it would, that was all it took to get a low growl out of Liam and a kiss that made every nerve ending in her body light up. He wrapped his arms around her and with an ease that she would never get tired of, he lifted her up. Reflexively, Bree wrapped her legs around him while they deepened the kiss.

There was another growl, only this one came from her.

More and more, her bear was growing insistent when it came to Liam. She wanted him. *All* of him.

Bree pushed her animal down, determined not to let her win. Instead, she focused on the man who held her easily with one arm, while his other hand worked at the clasp of her bra.

"Too. Many. Clothes." He grunted while his fingers deftly worked the snaps free.

Bree laughed. "I'm barely wearing anything."

"Still too much." He winked as he tore her bra from her body and released her heavy, full breasts into his hands. "Better." His nostrils flared as he looked hungrily at her tits. He moved her backward until he could drop her gently on the bed.

She scooted backward and leaned back on the quilt on her elbows, which she knew thrust her breasts up seductively.

Liam noticed and growled, a low rumble deep in the back of his throat.

"Mine." He stalked closer to the bed, his eyes focused intensely on hers. "Damn, I need you."

She grinned and narrowed her eyes. "Then take me."

LIAM DIDN'T HAVE to be asked twice.

In a flash, he tore her panties away and at once, his senses flooded with the sweet scent of her desire.

Damn. She was perfect. So responsive. So sexy. So...*everything.*

She's not yours,

his bear reminded him—just the way it had been on an increasing basis over the last few days.

He said he'd be patient with her and he'd meant it. But with every day that passed—hell, with every *minute* that passed—he understood less and less why they had to wait. She was *his.* He was *hers.* They both felt it. They both *knew* it. What was the purpose of waiting? It was driving him crazy. His bear could barely stand it.

Liam had heard stories about men whose bears grew restless, whose bears struggled inside them, threatening to destroy them from the inside out if they didn't answer their call. That was the thing about grizzlies: they wouldn't be denied. They were a powerful force that wanted what they wanted, and when they didn't get it, the results could be explosive.

Liam hadn't put enough stock in those stories. He'd thought for sure, he'd be strong enough to hold out so it wouldn't affect him. He'd been wrong.

He'd grown tired of being patient.

Maybe tonight?

Maybe.

The sweet scent of her arousal filled every part of him. His cock thickened almost to the point of being painful in his pants. He shed his clothes quickly and grabbed each of Bree's creamy-white legs in his hands. He ran his hands down the length of each gorgeous leg, until his thumbs joined together at the apex of her thighs.

She trembled under his touch and threw her head back as he used one thumb to circle her sensitive nub, while the other pressed gently, yet insistently, inside her.

"Liam." His name fell off her lips in a groan. "Ummm…" She couldn't formulate words, and he took great pride in that.

He bent and lowered his face between her legs, where he inhaled deeply before sucking her already throbbing clit into his mouth. It didn't take long for her to start squirming beneath his touch, but he held her firm with his big hands before running the width of his tongue down her creamy slit.

Bree cried out, and Liam knew she was close already.

So damn responsive.

He knew exactly how to make her scream.

That's because she's yours.

He ignored his bear and increased his attentions on the sexy woman in front of him. It didn't take long for her shudders to crest in an explosive orgasm. She cried out, uncaring who heard her. The fact that the others might overhear their lovemaking turned Liam on and he worked to draw out her climax.

Finally, Bree reached down and threaded her fingers into his hair to lift him up and away from her. His lips curled up in a satisfied smile. He'd never get enough of making her come like that.

But he wasn't done with her. His erection pulsed with a need of its own and despite the faraway look in Bree's eyes, Liam knew without a doubt he'd make her scream at least once more before the night was over.

He stood and licked his lips slowly before reaching out to lift Bree up off her back. His hands cupped and massaged each of her luscious breasts before traveling down to her hips.

"Let me see that gorgeous ass, babe."

She traced her tongue along the seam of her lips, but only for a moment before turning over so she was on her hands and knees.

The sight of her full, round ass made him groan out loud. "Every single inch of you is phenomenal." With his hands on her hips, he moved her backward until he was poised behind her, the tip of his erection pressing against her slick opening.

"I need you inside me."

Bree looked over her shoulder at him, and Liam didn't need more invitation than that. He pressed forward and drove into her hot, wet center.

Sheathed in her, he paused, letting himself enjoy every second of being with her.

But as much as he wanted to savor the moment, his bear had other plans. Plans that were out of his control.

Deep within him, his animal roared and took over. Liam took her hard and fast, and Bree's body responded to his attentions. She clenched around him, her second release imminent.

Instinct took over, and Liam folded himself over her, so his body almost covered hers. His mouth found the sensitive skin on the back of her neck and it was time.

He needed her to be his. He had to have her.

His mate.

He opened his mouth, his teeth bared.

Beneath him, he could feel Bree start to lose control as he continued to drive into her, taking her closer and closer to another orgasm. His bear took over and just as she let out her release, his sharp teeth pierced her skin.

Yes. Mine. My mate.

Liam closed his eyes. A rush of hot, satisfied heat flowed through his body as he slowly started to sink his teeth into her.

"No!" Bree shrieked and bucked beneath him. "Liam! Stop!"

The trance broken, Liam jerked backward, his teeth tearing away from his mate. But she wasn't his mate. Not yet. The process hadn't been completed.

The reality of what had happened—*almost* happened and not happened at all—slammed into him.

He stepped backward, away from her. His hand touched his lips and he shook his head. "Bree, I…"

On the bed, Bree had flipped over and backed up so she was pressed up against the headboard. Her breasts heaved with each quick, hard breath she took. On the air, Liam could still smell her arousal. But there was something else as well—fear.

She was scared of him.

No.

"Bree." He reached out his hand and took a step toward her. "I…I don't know what…I'm sorry." He tried to touch her, but she sucked her legs up tight and wrapped her arms around them. "Don't be scared, Bree."

"Stay away from me." Her eyes widened with terror.

Terror?

"Bree. It's me. I'm yours. I—"

"I told you no." Her voice shook and it killed him. "I wasn't ready. I told you, no. I *said* no."

"I know." Liam shook his head. "I know. You did and I

didn't..." He dropped his head and took a deep breath. "I'm so sorry, Bree. I shouldn't have pushed you like that. I know it's been a lot for you. So much to take in and...I never meant to hurt you. I just...well, I don't..."

"Get out."

His head jerked up. "What?"

She couldn't possibly mean to kick him out. They were fated. They were mates. Not officially. That was his fault. But still... it wasn't going to change what they were to each other. No. This was ridiculous.

"Bree."

"No, Liam." She pressed her lips together and shook her head. "I want you to leave. Please. Just respect this one thing."

Her words hit him like daggers. *He hadn't respected what she wanted. He'd hurt her.*

His bear struggled within him and Liam knew if he let it, his animal would disregard everything she'd just said, wrap her up in his arms, and not let her go until everything was okay again.

But his bear had gotten him into enough trouble for one night.

Liam took one last look at Bree, turned, and did what she asked.

He left.

Chapter Sixteen

"MERRY CHRISTMAS!"

Bree did a double take as she walked into the kitchen. *Had she missed a day? How was it Christmas already?*

"I…did I…" She looked around the room at the handful of people gathered there. "Is it Christmas morning?" she asked Nina as quietly as she could.

"Nope." Cyrus handed her a mug of coffee as he walked by. She nodded gratefully in his direction. Clearly, she needed more caffeine. "But it is Christmas Eve morning."

Bree almost cried she was so relieved. It had been a terribly long night. If she'd missed a day through all of her heightened emotions, she was pretty sure she would lose it completely. "That's not Christmas."

"Don't let Harper hear you say that," Chloe warned. "She's pretty convinced every day from December fifteenth to January first is Christmas." She rolled her eyes dramatically. "I'll be honest," she continued. "It's more festivity than I think I've had in my entire life combined."

"And you're loving every minute of it," Harper said as she

walked into the kitchen. "Don't even bother pretending you're not."

Chloe laughed. "You got me."

They teased, but even through her own sadness and confusion, Bree could appreciate the love between them all. A tear sprang to her eye, but she lifted her coffee mug and took a long sip before anyone could notice.

But someone *had* noticed. "Bree?" Ryker spoke up from the end of the eating bar, where he was perched on a stool. "Is everything okay this morning?"

She nodded but wouldn't look at the man.

"Are you sure? Because you know we're here if you need to talk about—"

"I'm good." She interrupted him, her voice sharper than she would have liked. "Sorry," she added with a mumble. "I'm just a little more tired than normal. I didn't get a great night's sleep last night."

Ryker looked her directly in the eye from across the room. "Neither did Liam."

Her heart clenched and she looked down at the dark liquid in her cup before she could burst out in tears.

"It's okay." Nina appeared at her side and wrapped an arm around her shoulders. "He's upset too."

Everyone else in the room had grown quiet, listening. But Bree didn't want to talk about it. Not really. How could she talk about something she couldn't even put into words? Because she couldn't. She couldn't for the life of her figure out why she'd reacted the way she had the night before.

Liam loved her. She loved him. She'd never in her life felt so strongly about someone. Hell, she hadn't even known it was possible. But it was. And with Liam she felt safe. With all of them. She felt safer than she ever had. Even when she was a little girl, tucked in between her grandparents and far away from the horror of her past…Liam felt safer than that.

So why did you kick him out?

She didn't know. Bree shook her head and let the tears fall down her cheek. Everything was so messed up.

"It's okay, Bree."

"No," she said to Nina. "It's not. It's not okay. None of it is."

"Liam is really upset," Nina said softly. "I know I'm not supposed to get involved..." She looked up toward Ryker, who nodded and got up from his stool.

"He came to our room last night," Ryker said. "It was after midnight. He was naked and covered in mud."

"Mud?" Alarmed, Bree looked around at the room, but no one else seemed concerned. "Is he...was he..."

"He's fine," Ryker explained as he took her hand and led her to the small table on the far side of the room. "He'd gone for a long, hard run along the ridge before he came to us. I'm not going to lie, I was surprised to see him. We haven't been all that close recently, but he was in a bad way."

Panic filled her. If she'd done anything to put him in danger, she'd never forgive herself. Sure, she was upset, but... she loved him. "Is he...? How is...oh no." She dropped her head into her hands.

"It's okay, Bree." Nina rubbed her back. "He just needed to talk things through."

"He's confused." Ryker spoke matter-of-factly. "I don't blame him, honestly." Bree's head shot up and she stared at him. Ryker held up his hands in defense. "Hey. All I'm saying is that for an alpha male grizzly who has found his mate and then be—"

"I hardly think you have any room to talk at all," Nina interrupted him. She had her hands on her hips and glared at her mate. "Don't you remember what happened between us?"

Instantly, Ryker's face fell and he shook his head. "That was different and I'm—"

"It wasn't different."

Ryker looked around the room, but everyone else, whether they agreed with him or not, was shaking their heads. No one dared to side with him on that one. He had been out of line with the way he and Nina had mated.

Nina, being full human, and not having any idea about shifters or how things worked, had been completely oblivious when Ryker had mated with her. It was against all of the grizzly clan codes to mate without permission, let alone without the partner not even being aware of what was happening. Nina hadn't even realized what had happened until it was explained to her by Harper and the other women. To say she'd been angry would be a massive understatement.

Maybe Liam was just like his brother?

No. That was different.

Bree shook her head. "I'm just not ready," she said out loud. "It's not that I don't love him, or even know that I want to be with him. I do. It's just...all of this, it's happened so fast that I'm still trying to work out what it all means."

From across the kitchen, Chloe nodded. "I totally get it. Besides, if you told him no..."

"No means no." Nina agreed. "Consent is important." She looked pointedly at Ryker, who moved to wrap his arms around his mate. He nuzzled her neck for a minute before looking up again.

"You're right," Ryker said. "Consent is consent and it's crucial. No matter what. Liam was wrong to do what he did," he said to Bree. "And he's hating himself for it right now. Will you talk to him?"

Bree opened her mouth but shut it again and shook her head. "No," she said after a moment. "I'm sorry he's upset and I appreciate the fact that he knows he screwed up, but I need some time. All of this is so much to take in. I mean, it was barely a week ago that I wasn't even *really* a shifter." She used her fingers to make air quotes. "And now my secret is out in the open, I'm shifting, I've started to get to know my bear and this whole new life." Bree looked around the kitchen at the people gathered there. They all cared about her. She knew that. But she also knew that Liam cared for her, too. And yet, he'd put his own needs and wants in front of hers.

Was that how it was?

If she couldn't trust him, who could she trust?

***

HE'D SCREWED UP. He knew that.

He'd spent the better part of the night going over and over it in his head. How he'd lost control. How he'd let his bear start doing the thinking for him.

It was a mistake.

It was a terrible mistake to let your animal take over. Everyone knew that.

He knew it. Yet, he'd still let it happen.

After he'd left Bree the night before, he'd spent the majority of the night running his bear to the point of exhaustion. After all, if the only way to get his animal to sit down and shut up was to make him tired, he'd do it. Because more than anything, Liam needed his bear to stay out of his life before he fucked it up completely.

It was late by the time Liam was satisfied that his bear might stay the hell out of his relationship. Naked, cold, and dirty, he returned to the Den. But with nowhere to go, and realizing that he couldn't just sleep on the couch where anyone could wake up and find him, he'd knocked on Ryker and Nina's door.

His brother's private cabin still wasn't completely finished, and they were staying in one of the guest rooms, just as Liam and Bree were. Well, the way Bree was. He knew he wasn't welcome in that room. At least not now.

Just remembering the fear on her face was almost enough to make Liam turn around and run his bear again. Hard. He'd punish himself over and over again for the way he'd made her feel. He didn't deserve her. Not if he scared her that way.

Fortunately, Ryker answered the door on the second knock before Liam could turn and go back outside into the cold night.

"Brother?"

"I screwed up." Liam dropped his head but stepped inside the room. He nodded in Nina's direction but immediately felt guilty for intruding on their night and turned to leave.

"Stay." Ryker put his hand on his bare shoulder before handing him a pair of sweats and a T-shirt.

"Stay." Nina nodded. "I was just going to get a cup of tea."

Liam didn't bother questioning why she'd get a cup of tea in the middle of the night; it was obvious she was trying to leave the brothers alone and he appreciated it more than he could say at the moment.

"What the hell's going on, Liam?" Ryker said the moment she was out of the room. "You're a mess."

"She kicked me out." Liam paced the floor. "I've ruined everything. Everything. I bit her and she told me no and—"

"Wait." Ryker stopped him. "You bit her?"

Liam nodded.

"You're mated? That's—"

"Don't say it." Liam stopped his brother. "It's not great. Nothing is great. She told me not to. She said she wasn't ready, and I did it anyway. And no, we're not mated. She kicked me out and now…" Liam dropped his head for a minute before looking up. "I can't blame her, though. I mean, that's who I am, right? I just do what I want. I take what I want. And I don't give a shit who gets in the way, or who I hurt."

Axel and Harper's wedding, Natalia, the clan…and now Bree.

"Whoa. That's a leap, don't you think?"

Liam stared at his older brother. "Is it?"

For a moment, Ryker didn't say anything, but finally he nodded. "It is. Liam, you're not that person anymore. Maybe once. But not anymore."

"People don't change."

"Don't they?" Something in his brother's voice had Liam turning around. "I did. Remember? I shared a lot of the same opinions as you about mates, and the clan and the old way. And what changed for me?"

"Nina."

"Right." Ryker nodded. "Nina changed it for me. But not before I almost fucked it up, too."

It was true. Ryker had mated with Nina without her even knowing who or what he was. It could have been catastrophic. But she forgave him.

"That's different." Liam shook his head stubbornly.

"You're right," Ryker said. "It *is* different because you changed *before* Bree came along. And while I'm definitely an advocate for how the love of a good woman can change everything, I can also give credit where credit is due. You've changed. A lot. And in a really short time."

Liam let his brother's words sink in for a while, but they still didn't resonate. Because all he could think of was his mate down the hall, and how she'd looked at him with fear in her eyes.

As much as his brother was trying to help, he couldn't understand Liam's situation. It was so different from what anyone else had gone through. The worst part was that all Liam wanted to do was protect Bree. From the moment he'd met her, he knew he wanted to keep her safe. And once she'd confided in him the truth about who she was, Liam knew without any uncertainty that it was his job to keep the Sterling clan from hurting her again.

That's all he wanted to do. And now he could do it. He could give her the information she needed to once and for all feel truly safe.

Ryker and Nina had been kind enough to let him crash in their easy chair for the rest of the night and after they'd gone down for breakfast, Liam helped himself to a quick shower and a change of clothes borrowed from his brother's drawer.

It was Christmas Eve and as much as he'd made a mess of everything—first by destroying the trust with his family...trust that he was working very hard on building up...and then, even worse, by blowing things up with Bree—he couldn't seem to stop himself. He just kept making things worse, when all he really wanted to do was fix things.

But as messy as things already were, there were about to get a whole lot messier.

Because when he'd been in Jackson Valley looking for information about the Sterling clan, he'd learned more than he'd bargained for. And instead of doing what he should have —come directly back and tell Bree everything—he'd made a deal.

And now that he'd put everything into motion, he had no idea how to stop it.

Chapter Seventeen

"YOU LOOK BEAUTIFUL, *MI AMIGA*." Ella reached up and took Bree's hand in hers as Bree finished up with the braid she'd been putting in Ella's long black hair.

"No, Ella." Bree smiled and shook off the compliment. "It's you who looks beautiful. Pregnancy has given you a glow. You really are stunning." It was true. Ella, always gorgeous with her slightly exotic features, had blossomed into a magnificently stunning woman. Bree didn't think it was possible for someone to get so much prettier, but Ella had proved her wrong.

The other woman laughed. "You're sweet," she said. "And don't get me wrong. I've loved this time." She rubbed her massive belly. "But I'm more than ready for this little one to come say hi. I'm so jealous of Kira right now."

Bree laughed. She didn't know how anyone could be jealous of the sleepless nights and the constant breast-feeding that Kira was doing, but the twins were pretty cute.

"Soon," Bree said. "Right?"

"Any day." Ella groaned. "Any minute, it feels like."

Bree put the hairbrush down and looked at her friend. "Any minute?"

Ella shrugged. "Probably not." She pushed up to a standing position. "With my luck, this baby won't be here until the New Year. But I do feel like it's close."

Bree laughed and walked with Ella to the door of Ella and Kade's cabin and pulled their jackets over their shoulders. It was a short walk to the Den, but it once more started snowing. She'd enjoyed the quiet time helping Ella get ready for the Christmas Eve festivities. It had taken her mind off how completely screwed up the rest of the day had been. Just over a week ago, she'd planned to spend the day before Christmas alone. Maybe cleaning up the store or taking care of some things that had been put off due to the busy season. But then, things had changed.

Everything had changed.

There was Liam.

And all of a sudden, Christmas had become about so much more. It had become all about the family she had never really had. Even when it was just her and her grandparents, she'd never had a big Christmas. Sure, her grandmother had tried to make it special. But she always felt as if something was missing.

Bree glanced down to her finger and her mother's ring that she'd taken to wearing. It had spent too long hidden away in the box. It was her gift to herself, to embrace her family heritage. For better or for worse.

She held Ella's hand as they made their way along the shoveled path to the main building. The sun had long set and the pathway was lit. With the snow falling around them, and the Christmas lights decorating the pine trees and the fences around the buildings, it felt as if they were in a Christmas snow globe. It hadn't even been twenty-four hours, but Bree couldn't help but miss Liam.

"Ella?" She stopped her friend as they made their way up

to the porch. "Do you think I was too hard on Liam?" As the day had worn on, she'd started to feel more than a little ridiculous about the way she'd reacted the night before. But at the same time, she was still upset. Her feelings were confused and she hadn't been able to think clearly all day.

"*Mi amiga.*" Ella tried to take her hands, but her enormous belly made it impossible for her to reach Bree. She shook her head in laughter and said, "There is no right or wrong. It's only how you feel that matters. But I will give you one piece of advice, if I may?"

Bree nodded. "Please."

"Listen to your bear. She knows more about what you need than you can even begin to understand."

Bree shook her head. She still didn't understand this *thing* inside her and how it could possibly know what was best for her.

"But there's one more thing," Ella said. "The most important."

"What's that?"

"It won't happen to you, *mi amiga.*"

"What?" Bree asked the question, but she knew what her friend was talking about. Even if she didn't want to admit it. "What won't happen to me?"

Ella tipped her head in sympathy. "I know it must be scary after what happened to your parents. But you can't live in fear of what *might* happen. Trust me, I know."

Bree let her friend's words soak in. Ella *did* know. When she'd met Kade and the rest of the Jacksons, it was because she was on the run from her clan in South America, where she'd been promised to a terrible man in an arranged marriage. She'd accepted a job as a cook at Grizzly Ridge under a false name and had been terrified of her own truth coming out, because of what it might mean.

That her clan would find her and harm her.

It was Ella's worst fear.

And they *had* found her. But Kade and the rest of the Jacksons had kept her safe. Just the way Liam had sworn to do.

"Ella…" Bree shook her head. "I'm so sorry. I forgot that you had gone through—"

"No." Ella cut her off. "Don't compare. We have different stories. They aren't the same, but the one thing I do know, no matter how different our backgrounds are, there is one thing that's the same."

"What's that?"

Ella's smile lit up her face. "The love of a Jackson." She winked. "Let him love you, *mi amiga*. It's worth it. And please, don't live in fear of what *could* be because you will miss out on everything that *will* be. And life is so good on the other side of fear." She put both hands on her belly and took a sharp breath as if to punctuate the point.

"Ella? Are you okay? Is it the—"

"I'm fine." Ella waved her away. "*Mi bebe* was only agreeing with me."

LIAM WAS OUT OF TIME.

Christmas Eve was upon them. The laughter of his family drifted up the stairs to where he'd been pacing in Ryker's room for the last hour. He'd spent the afternoon trying to reach his mother on the phone, but with the heavy snow clouds that had settled over the mountains, the cell service was spotty at best and no doubt, Jackson Valley was experiencing similar service issues. The wilds of Montana weren't known for their excellent cell coverage. A fact he normally enjoyed.

But there was nothing normal about what was about to happen. *Had it really only been yesterday when he'd thought it was a good idea to accept Tonia's request?*

It had.

And at the time, it hadn't seemed like a big deal to promise her a seat at their dinner table in exchange for helping him learn about the Sterling clan. Liam knew that Tonia would have told him whatever he wanted to know even without the promise of a favor. He could see it in her eyes. She wasn't a bad person. But she loved her children and she missed them. And they were locking her out.

So he'd agreed.

But now with the doorbell about to ring any minute to announce his mother and his aunt's arrival—an arrival that wasn't entirely welcome—he no longer thought it was a good idea. Because not only did Axel and Luke make it perfectly clear that they wanted to wait until after Christmas to reunite with the mother who'd abandoned them as young children, but the information that she had about Bree's history might not be as well received as he initially thought it might.

"Dammit, Liam." He glared at his reflection in the mirror over the dresser. "How could you be so stupid?"

He wasn't thinking straight—that was how. His bear, despite the hard run he'd given it the night before, was a mess. And he had been a mess ever since he met Bree.

Mates were supposed to clear your head, help you settle into yourself and your feelings. They made your instincts sharper, every feeling stronger and clearer.

Except when you denied them.

He clenched his fists at his sides and took a deep breath. He couldn't do anything about that now. Besides, even if he could, would Bree even want him anymore? *Had he destroyed her trust completely?*

He could fix it. *Yes.* The idea came to him in a flash. *How had he not thought of it before?*

Likely because with time running out, he was just grasping

at straws and desperate enough to take any idea that popped into his head.

It didn't matter.

Maybe he couldn't stop Tonia from showing up and the majority of his family hating him for ruining their holiday, but he could restore Bree's trust in him again. But the only chance he had at proving to Bree that he'd never do anything to hurt her was to tell her what he'd discovered before she heard it from someone else.

All he had to do was meet his mother and Tonia outside before they—

Fuck.

The chime of the doorbell reverberated through the house.

It was too late.

Chapter Eighteen

BREE HAD JUST ACCEPTED a glass of eggnog from Harper, who was dressed in a very festive red dress, when the doorbell rang.

"Who could that be?" Harper looked around the room. "We're all here."

Except Liam.

He'd been conspicuously missing most of the day. A fact that Bree both appreciated and hated. She needed the space from him to clear her head, but at the same time, she craved his presence.

"I certainly don't know," Bree finally said. "But whoever it is, I hope they have four-wheel drive because with that snow that's coming down, the roads are going to be crazy."

"Good point." Harper turned with a flutter of her skirt and ran over to answer the door, but Kade had beat her to it.

Bree watched along with everyone else as he swung the heavy wooden door open, but before she could see who stood there, something else caught her attention.

Liam.

The hairs on the back of her neck stood up, her heart beat

faster, and heat pooled between her legs. Bree turned slowly, and there he was.

It hadn't even been twenty-four hours, but she'd missed him with a physical ache that she hadn't even realized until she saw him again.

Her body moved instinctively toward him until she remembered why she'd been upset with him.

The feelings of hurt, betrayal, and distrust slammed into her as if she'd just walked into a wall.

He turned to her and for a moment, Bree was certain Liam would come to her, kiss her despite the fact that she wasn't sure whether she was still mad at him or not, and then everything would be back to normal again.

Easy.

Simple.

Not going to happen.

She was such a mess. Bree shook her head at her own ridiculousness. She wasn't a weak woman. She wasn't a woman prone to being indecisive or playing games or anything of the sort.

Except clearly she was.

She didn't even recognize herself lately.

Something needed to give. Swallowing her pride, Bree took a step toward Liam but before she could say anything, Kade's deep voice filled the room, pulling everyone's attention back toward the door and the new arrival.

"What the hell are you doing here?"

"Shit," Liam muttered under his breath and with a look of regret, shook his head, changed course and sprinted to the door, where he took the arm of a woman who looked vaguely familiar. Behind her was another similar-looking woman, but Bree had definitely not seen her before.

"Mom." Liam gave the woman a kiss on the cheek. "Merry Christmas." He turned to the other woman and reached for her hand, but not before Kade got between them.

"Oh no," he said. "This isn't happening right now." He crossed his arms and glared at the woman. "Not today. Not like this."

Axel and Luke appeared from the kitchen and stood next to their brother. Bree glanced around the room. Within moments, it had filled up with everyone. Well, not everyone... Kira and Nash were still absent. Judging by the tense situation at the front door, that was probably a good thing because Bree was starting to very quickly put the puzzle pieces together. There was only one woman who could get that type of reaction from Kade.

His mother.

Tonia.

"It's Christmas, Kade," Liam said. "Let's just—"

"Exactly," Kade interrupted him with a growl. "And if she thinks that just because it's a holiday that she can waltz back in here as if nothing happened all those years ago, then—"

"Kade," the woman pleaded. "Please. Give me a chance to explain."

Bree could feel the woman's pain all the way across the room.

"No." He shook his head. "There is—"

"Let her in." It was Axel who spoke. He stepped up, put a hand on his brother's shoulder, and pulled him gently back from the door.

But Kade shook him off violently. He spun and glared at his older brother. They were all alphas, but Axel was the clan leader, and despite his anger, Kade knew enough not to challenge him on this.

But he was clearly not happy.

"Come." Axel took his mother's hand and led her into the room.

Natalia went to greet her mother and accompany her inside as well.

But Bree only had eyes for Liam, who still stood next to the door. There was no doubt in her mind that he'd had something to do with Tonia's arrival tonight. And she wasn't the only one who thought so.

"This is your doing." Kade spun on Liam. "I don't know how, but I know you had something to do with this," he growled. "And just when I thought you'd changed, Liam."

"This has nothing to do with the past." Liam stepped up to him. "Nothing."

"I knew it. You only think of yourself." Kade's hands flexed into fists. His face grew redder by the moment. "Clan loyalty should come above all else." He shook his head. "But not for you, right?"

Bree stepped forward, afraid that Kade would hurt Liam, or worse. But what Liam said next stopped her in her tracks.

"Clan loyalty is important." He shook his head. "But nothing comes before the loyalty to my mate. Nothing. Not even my family."

My mate.

The words settled into her soul. *Even after the way she'd behaved, he still loved her. Wanted her.*

"I did this for her," Liam continued. "She needs answers. She *deserves* answers."

Answers? What answers?

Kade turned and locked eyes with Bree before his gaze traveled over to where his mother stood with Axel and Luke.

Tonia must have sensed him watching her. "Kade, please. It's not what you—"

Kade grunted, unwilling to hear anything she had to say, before he pushed past Liam and out the front door into the blizzard.

HE'D BEEN TOO LATE. Not that he really would have been able to do anything anyway. Besides, Liam thought as he watched Tonia talking to Axel and Luke, they were going to have to reunite sooner or later anyway.

Just because he was the one to facilitate it didn't make it any worse.

He glanced at the door where his cousin had disappeared, likely to run his bear and burn off some pent-up anger.

Well, maybe it did make it worse.

"He'll be okay." Bree touched his shoulder, and instantly Liam was soothed. He turned to see her beautiful face, screwed up in concern.

"Bree." Liam turned and took her hands in his. He needed to touch her, to feel her. To be close to her.

The last day without her was too much. He couldn't handle the distance between them. Never again.

"I'm so sorry, Bree. I don't know what I…I wish I hadn't…" He dropped his head and shook it slightly in a futile effort. The ability to form words or try to put exactly what he was feeling when it came to this woman was still completely beyond him.

She put her hand on his cheek and it was both the sweetest gesture as well as the most erotic.

Liam moved forward, needing to close the small amount of space between them. His need for her was beyond anything he'd ever felt before. All-consuming.

She shivered, but didn't move away. Still, Liam hesitated. His entire body revolted with the knowledge that he'd scared her. "I will never hurt you, Bree." He stared straight into her eyes. "Never."

"I know."

"I will wait a lifetime for you if that's what it takes. I

promise never to force you, never to rush you, and never to scare you again. Ever."

She opened her mouth to speak, but Liam was too consumed by the pain he'd caused her. Every time he closed his eyes, he could still see the fear in hers the night before. It killed him that he'd caused that. Even for a moment. He'd spend his whole life making up for it if that's what it took. He might have been that man before—the man who just took what he wanted —but he wasn't anymore.

"It's okay, Liam."

He shook his head. "No. It's not."

There was so much going on with Kristine and Tonia's arrival, so much he should be focused on considering he'd insti-gated the reunion. But the only thing he could focus on was Bree and the look in her eyes. The look that told him that he'd hurt her.

"Liam," she said again. "It is okay. You need to believe me when I tell you that." He looked away, unwilling to hear her, but she stopped him again. "I know you blame yourself for so much, but you need to stop. People can change. *You* have changed."

"You don't know." He shook his head. "You weren't here. You didn't see the way I—"

"I *do* know." She interrupted him. "Because I know you." Bree pressed a finger to his chest. "I know the real you. I *feel* you, and you're not the same person. Your family knows it, too. They love you and they forgive you. Now you need to do the same."

Liam swallowed hard. It was easy for her to say things like that. She hadn't almost ruined her entire family. She hadn't almost killed her sister and then…damn, he still hated himself for almost mating her without permission. He wasn't worthy of this. He shook his head hard and tried to turn away, but she stopped him.

"Listen to me." Her voice was quiet, but strong. "Enough is enough." He blinked hard. "I love you and I forgive you, Liam." Her words struck him in the heart. "Now it's time to let it go and move on. You're the only one here who's still holding onto the past."

He looked around the room and back to Bree. After a moment, he nodded. "You're right."

Her lips twitched up in a cocky grin. "I know."

The urge to pull her into his arms and kiss her until he believed in himself as much as she did was strong. *Very* strong. But there'd be time for that later. There was too much happening. Too much still that needed to be dealt with. Liam glanced over his shoulder to where Tonia was in deep conversation with Axel and Luke. He knew how much they had to discuss, how many feelings there would be that would need to be sorted out between mother and children. He was loath to break it up. As much as he wanted Bree to have the answers she was looking for, it could wait.

"Come," he said. "Have you officially met my mother?"

He led Bree over to the couch where Natalia, Cyrus, Nina, and Ryker were all gathered. After a bit of furniture rearranging, Liam pulled the love seat closer and the two of them sat down. "Mom," he said. "I think you might have met before, but I'd like to officially introduce you to Bree, my…"

"Mate." Bree held out her hand to Kristine.

But all Liam could do was stare, dumbfounded, at her.

"What did you—"

"I can't tell you how happy I am to meet you, Bree." Kristine stood and pulled Bree into a hug. "I look forward to getting to know you."

Liam's mouth opened and shut like a fish out of water. Bree turned and winked at him before sitting down and joining in the conversation with everyone.

"So none of you have met Tonia?" It was Nina who asked, and Natalia who shook her head.

"No. No one had."

"Not even me," Kristine said. "Which makes sense since I didn't even discover that I was a Jackson until after she'd left the clan."

"And when she came back?" Ryker asked. "Why didn't you guys tell us right away?"

Liam *had* known. But it didn't feel like his job to tell anyone. Although he had mentioned it to Axel and Natalia, it definitely hadn't been broadcast.

"She wasn't ready." Kristine shrugged apologetically. "She wasn't sure how the children would feel to have her back. And then with Dad dying….it was a lot. It's been a lot."

Everyone nodded in understanding, but it still didn't make sense to Liam. "I guess the important thing is that she's here now and she can explain it to them." He gestured with his head. "They're the ones who matter here."

"Exactly," Kristine said. "And I think they will understand. After all, I think all of us know that sometimes things aren't so black and white when it comes to being a grizzly shifter and dealing with clan law." She looked directly at Bree when she spoke, and Liam instinctively reached for her hand.

He still couldn't be sure how she was going to react to finding out the truth about her clan and what had happened when she was a child. But what he did know was that she needed to know for sure. She deserved the truth. No matter how painful it might be.

"Kristine!" Harper arrived with baby Lily strapped to her back and a tray of drinks in her hand. "Merry Christmas. I haven't seen you in ages."

"Congratulations on your wedding," Liam's mother said genuinely. "I heard it was a special day."

Ryker snorted and Natalia threw a look in his direction, but

Liam only shook his head. It was true that Liam had been totally out of line at Axel and Harper's wedding. He'd tried to stop it, not believing at all in the human tradition of marriage. Fortunately, Ryker had stopped him, but not before Liam almost sabotaged his brother's relationship with Nina.

Damn. There really were a lot of reasons for his family to be upset with him.

Of course, that was before. Things had changed. A lot.

"Well, I'm glad you're here," Harper said, expertly steering the conversation away from the tender topic. "Will you join us in the remainder of the Reindeer Games?"

"Are we still doing that?" Liam groaned. "I just thought that with everything all…well, with Mom and Tonia here…"

"The more the merrier." Harper grinned. "Besides, tonight is the grand finale event."

They all exchanged wary glances, but it was Bree who was brave enough to ask. "What's the grand finale, Harper?"

"Christmas karaoke!"

Liam couldn't help it; he burst out in laughter, but only for a moment before he realized the room had grown quiet. Everyone was staring in the direction of the front door and Kira, who'd just walked in.

BREE'S HEART broke for her friend and her first instinct was to run to her and shield her from the emotions she was about to feel. A bond between mother and daughter was strong and Bree knew all about how much pain Kira had felt surrounding her mother's abandonment.

But Bree had expected her friend to yell or scream, or tell Tonia to leave the way her twin brother had. Instead, she surprised everyone. Kira's eyes had locked onto Tonia's the moment she entered the room, and now it was as if a magnet existed between the two of them, pulling them ever closer together.

Bree, along with everyone else in the room, watched the two of them, completely transfixed.

They moved slowly, ever closer until finally Tonia opened her arms. Kira walked straight into her mother's embrace and held her as if her life depended on it.

Maybe they should have felt as if they were intruding on a private moment, but no one could look away as the women both broke down into sobs that shook their bodies. Still at the door, Nash picked up the baby carriers and slowly moved into the room to get them in from the draft of the door. But other than that, no one moved while mother and daughter shared their reunion.

Bree couldn't be sure how much time had passed, before Luke and Axel joined them in a group hug. The family was once more complete.

Except Kade.

Bree ached for her friend. He was so stubborn, so hard-headed and so hot-tempered, it often backfired on him in the worst way. Bree knew that Kade only meant to protect his sister and the rest of his siblings from further hurt, but sometimes he needed to look past his own walls in order to see the truth of a situation.

It was something Ella had helped with immensely. But still, there was work to do.

The thought of Ella had Bree looking away from the family reunion and around the room for her pregnant friend. But she was nowhere in sight.

When had she seen her last?

Bree turned slowly, but Ella wasn't there. Without saying a word, Bree stood and moved as quickly as she could to the kitchen.

"Ella?" She looked around the empty kitchen, but Ella

wasn't there either. *Surely she hadn't gone after Kade? Not in the storm? Not in her condition?*

She turned to leave. *Maybe she'd gone up to her cabin for something.* Just as Bree was about to push out the door back into the living room, a sound grabbed her attention. She spun on her heel, but still, no one was there. "Ella?" She called out again, but this time her voice was little more than a whisper. A completely unfounded fear gripped her by the throat. Her heart thudded in her chest.

Something was wrong. Had they found her? Her clan?

"No!" She yelled the word aloud, angry at herself for even allowing a second of entertaining such ridiculous thoughts. She was safe. Her clan was not going to find her. She was *not* in danger.

Never again.

Her thoughts flashed to the man in the other room. The one who just the night before she'd been so unreasonably afraid of. But just as soon as the image of Liam's face filled her mind, it all became clear.

It had never been *him* she was afraid of. It had never been *mating* she'd been scared of. It hadn't even been the fact that everything was happening and changing so fast that was making her pause. She hadn't been worried that her clan would find her. No, not really. Not when she was really honest with herself. And it was long past time she was honest with herself. Because the only thing that Bree had really been afraid of was her own heart.

What if, just like her parents, she gave in to the desires of her heart, and lost herself because of it?

After all, her parents had died for their love. They would still be here if they hadn't have allowed themselves to follow their heart.

Bree almost laughed aloud as the realization became clear. She'd been so stupid. So foolish. And so completely blind.

Because it was true that her parents died because of the love they shared, but that hadn't been their fault. They couldn't control old patriarchal views on mating that didn't support their love. All they could really do was follow their hearts, because a life lived without love was no life at all.

Her heart clenched in her chest. Thank God she'd realized her mistake while there was still time to fix it.

A weight lifted from her shoulders. She pulled her shoulders back and a smile lit up her face.

She had to find Liam. *She had to tell him. She had to—*

"Bree?"

The small voice stopped her cold and at once, the smile fell off Bree's face, all senses on alert.

———

BREE SPUN around and dashed to the other side of the counter in search of the voice.

"Ella!"

There, in a pool of liquid on the tile floor, barely propped up against the cupboards, was her pregnant friend. Her eyes were squeezed shut, her breathing labored. If Bree hadn't been so sure she'd heard Ella call her name, she never would have believed it. The other woman was so completely inwardly focused, Bree couldn't even be sure she recognized her presence.

Bree knelt on the floor. Her dress soaked through with liquid Bree didn't want to think about. "Ella? Are you okay? Is it the baby?"

Of course it was the baby. Bree shook her head and grabbed Ella's hand. Instantly, Ella squeezed down with a strength she didn't know the small woman could possibly possess.

A second later, Ella clenched her teeth and made a guttural

noise that sounded as if it had come from the depths of her very soul.

Bree's eyes widened. She'd never seen a baby born before, but it didn't take a medical expert to realize that Ella's baby was coming.

Quickly.

"Help!" She turned her head and yelled toward the door, hoping desperately that someone heard her over the chatter and Christmas carols in the other room because there was no way she could leave Ella's side. Not even for a second. Bree called out one more time before turning inward and focusing on her connection with Liam. Bree had no idea how it worked. But she did know there was some kind of mate bond. Did it only work if they were actually mated? She didn't know. There was no way to know for sure. But she had to try.

Liam! Help. I'm in the kitchen.

She only had time to focus once, quickly, before Ella demanded her attention again. She still hadn't opened her eyes, but she was breathing rapidly, in short, shallow breaths, her chest heaving, her stomach visibly contracting. Again, she bared down and let out a long, low grunt.

It was too soon.

Weren't the contractions supposed to be further apart? Was she pushing?

Bree shook her head. "No. No. No."

"Bree?"

"I'm here!" She popped her head up and called out at the sound of Liam's voice. "It's Ella," she said as Liam came into view on the other side of the massive kitchen cupboards. "The baby. Get help." There was no time for complete sentences, and Liam didn't seem to need them.

Without another word, he ran off and a moment later, the kitchen was full of voices and people.

Bree shuffled around to get out of the way as Tonia

dropped to her knees in front of Ella. "I've delivered dozens of babies. Do you trust me?"

There was no response from Ella, who was still turned so completely inward, so it was Bree who answered. "Absolutely."

Tonia met her eyes and for a moment, Bree was sure she saw a flash of something else in the stranger's look. *Love? Compassion?*

There was no time to think any further. Bree moved until she was behind Ella, supporting her and holding each of her hands. Tonia barked out a list of orders and the rest of the room ran off to get her what she needed, but Bree didn't pay anyone else any attention. Instead, she was completely focused on her friend and helping her get through such an important moment of her life.

"The baby is coming," Tonia announced. "Now." She turned and looked at Liam, who still stood behind her, waiting for his instructions. "Where's Kade?"

Liam shrugged, and for the first time, Ella spoke. "Kade." His name came out as a plea and Bree's heart broke a little. Kade needed to be here.

Both Bree and Tonia stared at Liam and spoke at the same time. "Get Kade."

Bree wanted to say more. She wanted to tell him to hurry, that there wasn't much time, that the baby was almost there. But a moment later, Ella let out a piercing scream, and everyone turned their attention back to her and the baby who was about to make an entrance into the world.

When Bree looked up again, Liam was gone.

LIAM WAS TEARING off his clothes as he ran through the living room, so by the time he hit the snow-covered porch, he was already half naked. He leapt off the porch, his pants shredding around him as he shifted. He hit the ground in a cloud of soft, powdery snow and immediately started running in the direction of the ridge.

There was one place where the Jackson men could reliably be found running their bears when they needed to let off steam.

The ridge.

As Liam ran, pushing his body to the max, he tried to reach out to his cousin.

Telepathy between mates was strong. Almost effortless. Stronger still when they were mated.

Siblings, particularly twins, had a very strong connection as well. But the connection fell off noticeably after that. Cousins had been known to share a connection, particularly when they were close, but Liam was definitely not one of Kade's favorite people at the moment. The odds that Kade would *hear* his calls were slim.

Liam tried anyway.

Kade! Emergency. Baby. Ella.

He kept his messages pointed and repeated them over and over as he ran toward the ridge. The snow was falling so hard, he almost didn't see the alpha grizzly barreling toward him at top speed until he was upon him.

At the last minute, Liam veered to the side, tripped over a log, and rolled into the snow before landing on all four feet again.

You okay? Can't stop.

Kade's voice filled his head. Liam smiled to himself and immediately started running after his cousin.

I'm fine. Go. She needs you.

Kade only seemed to pick up speed, fueled by the need to get there for his mate and his baby. Liam had no hope in catching him. Still, he pushed himself so he was right behind him as Kade leapt to the porch, shifting as he went, and in what looked like one seamless move, opened the front door to the Den and slipped inside.

Liam laughed as he, too, shifted, picked up the shreds of his ruined pants and went inside.

The Den was abuzz with activity and excited chatter when he entered.

"I'd offer you a blanket, brother," Ryker said. "But I gave it to Kade. You guys sure are hard on pants."

Liam rolled his eyes, but no one thought anything about family members walking around naked. That was the thing about a shifter family. "Be right back." Liam jogged upstairs to the room he'd been sharing with Bree. He inhaled deeply, taking in her scent and the lingering scent of their lovemaking that still clung to the bedclothes. He still hadn't had a chance to talk to her properly. To make things right. But he would. And they'd be back here in this room. Once again he'd hold her in his arms. And this time, he was never letting go. Not for anything.

Chapter Nineteen

BABY NOEL WAS BORN QUICKLY and besides the fact that he was born on the kitchen floor—without incident; a healthy eight-pound boy—no one could quite believe that such a petite woman had produced such a robust baby boy.

Except Bree.

She'd been there through the whole thing. Even after Kade arrived, naked and wrapped in a blanket, his eyes wide—she'd stayed. She couldn't have left if she'd wanted to because only one push later, little Noel came into the world with a scream.

Bree sat in wide-eyed wonder at what had just happened, and despite it all, how easy Ella had made it look.

"It's a boy." Tonia held the newborn, her grandson, for a moment before quickly wrapping him in a clean towel someone had brought. "Your son, Kade." She handed him the infant with a smile that brought tears to Bree's eyes.

It had barely been an hour earlier that Kade had yelled at his mother and run off. Now, the connection that passed between the two of them was undeniable.

"Thank you." He spoke softly and took the baby in his arms.

For the first time since the ordeal in the kitchen had begun, Ella opened her eyes and stared at her new little family with so much love in her eyes that it made Bree weep openly.

She met Tonia's eyes, also full of unshed tears and more emotion than Bree could comprehend. Tonia nodded and together, the two women got up and slipped out of the kitchen to give the new family a little time to get to know each other.

Now, a few hours later, the kitchen had been tidied up, the new little family moved to the comfort of one of the guest rooms so Ella could rest, and Zoe and Gabe were in the kitchen with Gabe's son Ashton, pulling together whatever snacks they could find for a Christmas Eve dinner.

It was almost as if the chaos of Noel's dramatic birth had served to bring everyone together, and now that it was behind them, a calm settled over the Jackson family. Bree snuggled close to Liam on the couch, thankful for his warm support.

Christmas carols played softly and despite the fact that it was still relatively early in the evening, Bree closed her eyes and felt herself drift off. But she couldn't have been asleep for very long when Liam shook her shoulder gently and whispered in her ear. "Bree? Tonia and I need to tell you something."

She blinked slowly and let Liam's face come into focus as she processed what he'd just said. "Tell me something?" She looked first to him and then to his aunt, who stood in front of them. She was a beautiful woman, Bree realized for the first time. She looked so much like Kira, but with a little silver around her temples, and a few more lines on her face. Maybe from the stress of being away from her children.

Tonia had explained to all of them earlier, that when she'd made the choice to leave the children with her father and the Jackson clan, it truly was the decision she felt was best for them. It was no life to watch your father die, and Tonia wouldn't, couldn't, leave him to die alone. She wished things had been different, she'd said. But she would have made the same choice again and none of her children could disagree with that. Each of them had now experienced fated mates and the strength of the connection. Even now that Kira, Axel, and now Kade, had children. They understood the need to do what was best for your children, and none of them could disagree that growing up in the Jackson clan hadn't been a good experience. Besides, that was the past and the important thing was to look forward to the future. As a family.

"Bree?"

Still half asleep, she'd been lost in her own thoughts and almost closed her eyes again. Liam roused her and she sat up with a bashful smile. "Sorry." She shrugged. "I didn't realize I was so tired."

"It was a pretty exciting evening," Tonia said. Bree slid over a little so the other woman could sit on the edge of the couch with her. "And you were absolutely fantastic."

"No." Bree shook her head. "It was Ella. I've never seen anything like that. She was so focused."

Tonia nodded. "I've only seen that once or twice before. It's as if the mother turns inward and puts all their love and energy into the child in order to get through the experience. It's pretty incredible. Ella's pretty incredible." She smiled kindly and took Bree's hand. "But you were too. You really were. She was lucky to have you there."

"We're all pretty lucky to have her." Liam wrapped his arm around her and squeezed her close to him. "She's family."

Bree reveled in the love she felt from him and when Tonia spoke again, she was grateful for his strength.

"More than you know, Bree."

Automatically, Liam's arms tightened a little around her.

"I don't understand." She glanced back at Liam and then to Tonia again, a hard knot of fear in the base of her stomach. "What are you talking about?"

"Remember when I told you I was going to get you some answers about the Sterling clan? *Your* clan?"

She nodded. Of course she remembered. He'd gone to Jackson Valley to talk to—*Tonia? But what would she know?* The older woman was watching her, trying to measure her reaction, but to what, Bree still didn't know. Tonia's eyes drifted down to the ring Bree wore. Her mother's ring.

"What do you know?"

Did she want to know? Was it better to live in ignorance as to who and what her clan was? After all, they'd murdered her parents. Would they come after her?

She took a deep breath and squeezed her eyes shut for a moment before asking again. "What do you know?"

———

LIAM COULD FEEL Bree's fear. She trembled in his arms, but also she was brave and he loved her even more for the strength she had running through her.

"My mate, the father of my children," Tonia began with a sad smile. "He was a Sterling."

"What?" Bree tensed in his arms. "What do you mean?"

He could feel her heart rate increase, but he held her tight, needing her to feel the safety in his arms.

"In fact," Tonia continued, "he was your uncle. Your mother, Lucy, was his sister. You look just like her."

Bree shook her head. "No," she said. "That's not possible."

"It is." Tonia took her hand and squeezed gently.

"Am I in danger?" She sat up, pulling away from Liam's embrace. She immediately felt his absence but the panic that had begun to course through her wouldn't be settled. She needed to move.

Bree was about to jump to her feet when Tonia put a hand

on her arm. "You're not in danger," she said kindly. "I promise. You aren't in danger. And you never were."

The older woman's words took a moment to sink in, but when they did, Bree shook her head. "What do you mean, I never was?" It didn't make sense. Nothing made sense. "I was always in danger. I had to hide who I was. I had to pretend to be someone I wasn't. Something I wasn't. My clan…the Sterlings, they—"

"Always loved you." Tonia spoke softly and with so much honesty, Bree couldn't help but believe her. "You were always wanted. You were always loved. The Sterling clan grieved the loss of you and your parents for years. It was a terrible tragedy what happened to them. Bree, I'm so sorry."

"None of this makes sense. My grandparents…they ran away with me. They saw my parents killed. By their own clan. They saw it…they watched it." She could hear her voice growing more and more frantic. She knew she needed to calm down. She needed to breathe and let the woman tell her the story, but deep inside her, her bear warned her with a low rumble. Did she *really* want to know the truth? *Didn't she already know? Really?* "Tell me." She sat back hard and looked up to Tonia, who was waiting patiently for Bree to calm down.

"No one really knows the exact chain of events," she started as soon as Bree was calm. "But the best that they can figure is that the couple you know as your grandparents, who were once the Raymonds before they changed their names to Brooks—befriended your parents when you were very young. Your mom and dad had moved into town, away from the clan to be closer to their jobs so they could spend more time with you. Your mom knew how important it was to have close bonds. And from everything I've ever heard about her, she loved you more than anything else in the whole world." Her voice grew far away for a moment before she refocused and continued. "The Raymonds had never been able to have children of their own and when your family moved in, they fell in love with you. That much you should also know. They loved you very much."

Bree nodded. "But I thought my parents had fled their clan because they didn't want them to be together?" She shook her head, but there was nothing in Tonia's eyes that would reveal a lie. Nothing but the truth was reflected back at her. "I thought they'd run away."

"No," Tonia said. "In fact, the Sterlings believed they told you that as part of an elaborate story to explain things to you."

"What does that mean?"

You know. You've always known.

Bree swallowed hard and pushed her bear down in an effort to silence her.

"The Raymonds staged the whole thing," Tonia began. "Once they knew who you were, and *what* you were, they'd decided to spare you from such a life." Tonia shook her head wryly. "Of course, they didn't have any idea about what kind of life they were really *saving* you from. But they thought they were doing the right thing, taking you from your parents."

"But they...no..." Bree couldn't say the words out loud. Surely, even if the Raymonds had conspired to kidnap her and make up an elaborate story, they never would have killed her parents. "They loved my mom and dad. I *know* they did. You don't just fake that kind of thing. I know it."

Tonia took her hand and squeezed. "They didn't mean to kill them," she said slowly. "They didn't mean for them to get hurt at all. It got out of hand and they panicked."

"Panicked?"

Tonia nodded. "From what we understand, the plan was to stage a break-in and, in the confusion, take off with you. They planned on starting a new life with you and raising you as their own grandchild."

"They did that." Bree was numb. She couldn't feel her feet.

Nothing felt real. But she couldn't shut down. She needed to know everything. "But my parents—they died."

Bree felt Liam's arms around her again, holding her safe.

Tonia nodded slowly and absently. "That wasn't supposed to happen. The Raymonds hired some local thugs. They turned out to be from a nearby wolf pack. Rogues, actually. But of course, the Raymonds wouldn't have known anything about that. The wolves realized they'd been hired to *scare* shifters, so they scared them, all right." Tonia looked down at her feet. "Apparently it happened very quickly. The Raymonds panicked. Grabbed you and ran. You were scared and rightly so. In fact, it only strengthened their resolve to never let you experience that lifestyle. They wouldn't risk losing you to such a violent end, so they made up an elaborate story, took you far away and…"

"I had no idea."

"How could you?"

A small, salty tear slid down her cheek. She squeezed her eyes shut and tried to remember the events of that night. But the only thing she could remember was being scared. *So* scared. And the screams. So she ran. She grabbed her stuffed toy, the ring that had rolled down the hall from her mom's finger, and she ran to the Raymonds.

Who'd been ready and waiting.

As if they knew.

Because they *did* know.

All the pieces clicked together and in an instant it all made sense.

The way the Raymonds had been packed, the car running. The clothes they had already bought for her. They'd been prepared for her to come over for help. Months of grooming her, training her, making sure of what the result would be beforehand.

But they hadn't known what would happen.

Bree squeezed her eyes shut. But when she did, all she could see was the blood, her father's face as he told her to run.

"How could they do that?" She looked frantically between Liam and Tonia, as if they held the answers. "I don't understand. They loved me. They loved my parents. They wouldn't do this." Tears flooded her eyes, and she hated herself for it.

It was Tonia who grabbed her hands and looked her straight in the eyes. "They did love you. Very much. Never doubt that."

How could she *not* doubt it?

"You can't know that."

"I can," Tonia said. "Because Mrs. Raymond sent a letter almost two years after the incident. That's the only reason we know the real events of that night. Although, there were rumors."

"They sent a letter? To you?" Nothing made sense. Bree shook her head in an effort to clear her thoughts, but it didn't work. She couldn't imagine ever being able to make sense of all this.

"To the family," Tonia answered. "It seems she had an attack of conscience and felt absolutely terrible about how things went down. She explained that her love for you, both of their love for you, was more than they could bear and once they knew who you were, *what* you were, they had convinced themselves that they were doing good by taking you. Like I said, they never intended for your parents to get hurt. The guilt ate them up and I think that despite the bad choices they made, they were good people. Just a little misguided. It was important for the clan to know that you were okay."

"But if the clan knew I was alive," Bree started, "then why didn't they...how could they just..."

"Mark told me that they left you where you were because you were so young. It was all you knew. There was no point disrupting you again. But they checked on you from time to time. They wanted to make sure you were happy and safe."

Flashes of people's faces—teachers, strangers in the store, Scout leaders over the years who'd come into her life and taken a special interest in her…were they…*they were.* Bree nodded. "There were people." She turned and spoke to Liam. "Not always, but every once in a while, I'd meet someone and feel like I'd known them forever, like they were part of me."

"Because they were part of your clan."

She turned back and leaned into Liam behind her, suddenly exhausted. "This is all so much."

Liam rubbed her arms and murmured softly into her ear. She didn't know what he said, but it didn't matter because he was there for her. That's all that mattered. She knew that now more than ever. Her family, her birth family, was gone. The people she thought were her grandparents, were gone. Physically and now emotionally. How could she ever think of them the same way again now that she knew what the truth was?

She took a deep breath and let it out slowly.

"I know this is a lot to take in," Tonia said gently. "When Liam came to me and asked me what I knew about the Sterling clan, I was shocked. Especially when he told me who you were. It's important to remember that through all of this, everyone loved you. And right or wrong, the choices that were made, they were made out of love, Bree."

***

IT WAS A LOT. A real lot. But it wasn't too much. Liam could see the toll it was taking on Bree to learn the truth about her family.

But he could also see that she could handle it.

She was strong. Unbelievably strong.

He was so proud of her. After speaking to Tonia, and

hearing everything she had to say, Liam had led Bree outside onto the porch. Wrapped in a blanket, Bree stood and stared out into the darkness at the snow falling down all around them. She didn't speak for a while, but Liam didn't rush her. She had a lot to process.

After a few minutes, she spoke without turning his way. "I think I always knew."

"About your parents?"

She nodded. "Well, more about my grandparents. I always had a feeling. Maybe it was my instinct."

"It probably was."

"But I always felt like there was something they weren't telling me. Like they knew more about what had happened that night than they'd said. I think I always knew that they'd had something to do with it."

Liam nodded despite the fact that she wasn't looking at him.

"But I didn't want to know." She turned then. "Does that make sense?"

"It makes perfect sense." He moved closer to her, wanting to give her the space she needed to work through her feelings, but also wanting to be there for her. "When you know your whole life can change in an instant, I absolutely understand how you'd want to work to keep that from happening. Of course."

"I still love them."

He slipped an arm around her. "Of course you do."

"And I don't hate them. Maybe I should," she added. "But I don't. I don't think I ever could."

"I think that's perfectly okay." He nuzzled the back of her neck and asked her the question he'd been avoiding. "And me?"

"You what?" She leaned back against him.

"Do you hate me?" He swallowed hard. "For bringing this to you. On Christmas Eve."

"Liam!" Bree spun around so quickly in his arms, he was almost knocked backward. "Why would I *ever* hate you? I love you."

He'd never heard the words from her mouth before and despite the fact that he'd felt them from the moment they'd met, hearing them fall from her delectable lips was more poignant than he ever could have imagined. "You love me?"

"You know I do." She smacked him lightly on the chest.

"But everything that happened. When I…" He shook his head, still angry that he'd tried to mate her without her permission. "I'm so sorry, Bree." He traced a finger down her cheek and cupped it in his hand. "I will never hurt you. I would never." He kissed her hard. "Ever."

"I know." Her smile was so sweet. So trusting. So completely his. She kissed him back, this time dropping the blanket so it fell to their feet. "I want to be yours. Completely."

"You are mine," he started. "I don't—"

"No." She stopped him. "Completely. I want to mate with you."

"You do?"

"More than anything." She kissed him again, this time pressing her body against his in a way that had his body responding with an urgency he'd never felt before. He would happily make her his, right here, right now.

Behind them, inside the warmth of the main room, Liam could hear the strains of "Jingle Bells" being sung—very poorly—as the last event of Harper's Reindeer Games kicked off.

He shook his head reluctantly. There was no way they could do it here. Nor would they be able to successfully sneak past their family to get upstairs.

"Baby, there is nothing more that I want than to take you…" An idea flashed in his head. It wasn't the most romantic idea, and he silently vowed he'd make it up to her. But desperate times called for desperate measures. "Are you serious about this?" He looked straight into her eyes, and there was no trace of uncertainty.

Bree nodded with a smile. "I've never been more serious about anything."

That was all he needed to hear. Liam took her hand and they took off running. Down the steps of the porch and into the deep snow, across the yard to the adventure center.

Chapter Twenty

"YOU CAN'T BE SERIOUS?" Bree shook her head, but she was laughing because Liam *was* serious. They'd snuck into the adventure center on the other side of the yard.

As soon as they were inside, Liam spun around and pushed her against the wooden wall. "Oh, I'm dead serious, baby. I've wanted this from the moment I laid eyes on you, and every moment since without making you mine has only intensified that." He kissed her. "I want you." Again, this time the kiss was lower on her neck. "I love you." His hands came up under her sweater and cupped her breasts. "I need you."

She vibrated from her own need that had only been building in intensity. The other day when she'd pushed him away, she'd been wrong. So very wrong. But that didn't matter, because now she had him and he would be hers. They would be mated.

"God, I need you." She went straight for his belt buckle and yanked it free before tearing the buttons of his jeans away and pushing them down. When his pants were around his ankles, it was her turn to kiss him.

With her mouth on his, Liam somehow managed to tug her

leggings down, so she could step free of them. But they got hung up on her boots and Bree laughed as she broke free from his embrace.

"I guess we need to slow down a bit." She bent down to pull first her boots off and then her leggings. When she stood upright again, Bree laughed once more because Liam was completely naked.

"That wasn't quite the response I was looking for." He pretended to be offended. "You don't like what you see?"

She narrowed her eyes and sucked her bottom lip between her teeth. "Oh, baby. Believe me, I like every long, hard inch of what I see." As she closed the gap between them, Bree pulled her sweater off over her head and released her breasts from the confines of the bra she was wearing. Liam's pupils dilated as he took in all of her.

She would never grow tired of seeing how much he wanted her.

"Woman, you are going to kill me."

She ran her hands up his solid chest of muscle. "I can think of worse ways to go."

Liam growled, a sound that came from deep within him. A moment later, his hands were on her ass, gripping her and lifting her. She wrapped her bare legs around him and used her strength to pull herself against his hard cock. It throbbed with need against her, and her own moisture pooled between her legs.

The combined scent of their mutual arousal filled the air and despite the fact that they'd barely even touched, Bree was sure her orgasm was imminent.

In a mutual understanding, Liam backed her up against the wall, his mouth locked on hers, their tongues tangled in an erotic dance. It wasn't until he had her pinned that he pulled back and looked at her. "You know how this works, right?"

The mating.

Bree nodded. She knew enough from her friends that he would bite her at the moment she climaxed and then she would be his. She was ready. She wasn't scared. But there was one more thing. Something not all of the females did. "I want to make you mine, too."

Liam's eyes clouded with shock, but only for a moment before they cleared again and he grinned. "You know this makes me yours, too."

"I know. But I want more. I want it all." She swallowed hard, as the decision she'd only just made crystallized in her mind. "I want to bite you."

Against her, Bree could feel his cock thicken and pulse against her. He liked the idea, too.

"Baby, I can't think of anything sexier than you taking me as your own." He kissed her to punctuate his point as he lifted her slightly, before lowering her onto him in one solid thrust.

SHE DROPPED her head back with a groan as he entered her. Just as it was every time they came together, Liam had to take a minute to control himself. He wanted her hard and fast and although this particular lovemaking session was going to be just that, it also was going to be the most important time they came together.

Bree was already close before they started. Her arousal filled his senses, and it didn't take long before she began to tremble around him. "Okay, baby. Are you ready?"

She nodded but kept her eyes squeezed shut. "I want you," she groaned. "Make me yours."

He didn't need to be asked twice. Seconds later, as Bree began to come apart around him, he dipped his head down to her neck. He kissed and sucked the skin there until she was wriggling in his arms, all but screaming as her climax took hold.

But that wasn't where he wanted to leave his mark. Quickly, he moved his mouth lower, between her full, gorgeous breasts and just as Bree screamed out her release, he bit down.

It was the most erotic thing he'd ever experienced, and his own orgasm threatened, but he had to hold off. Bree wanted to make her mark, too. And there was no way he would deny her that. Hell, he wouldn't deny her anything.

Liam waited, holding himself back while she recovered from her climax. When he felt her body still beneath his, Liam finally sat up. He licked his lips and kissed her, the taste of her on him.

"My turn." She grinned and licked her lips. "Are you ready?"

He moaned and thrust up inside her. "I thought you'd never ask."

Her body hugged him tight as Liam increased his pace. He drove into her, over and over until he felt his own release near. But so did Bree. Reading him perfectly, she ran her hands down his chest, and tweaked each nipple in turn. He growled and held her tighter and then, just when Liam didn't think he could take one more moment, she whispered, "Now."

His entire body shuddered and on the edge of his orgasm was the slightest sting of pain as Bree bit down on his shoulder. But it only intensified the climax in a way he never could have expected.

He let himself go. Threw his head back and roared out as she made him hers.

Forever.

Chapter Twenty-One

WHEN BREE OPENED her eyes the next morning, it was still dark. But the happy squeals of a little boy on Christmas morning would wait for no one. Ashton was only six and considering it was Gabe and Zoe's first Christmas together as a new family, *Santa* may have gone a little over the top. Not that Bree minded the early morning wake-up call. Not at all, because it meant spending more time with her new mate.

Mate.

She smiled lazily and rolled the word around in her mind. She didn't think she'd ever get sick of the way it sounded. But she knew for sure she would never grow weary of how it made her *feel.*

She stretched her arms over her head and relished in every sore muscle, caused by not only their mating session, but also the night full of fun activities they'd enjoyed. They'd finally escaped the Christmas Carol Karaoke after showcasing their skills in "Rockin' Around the Christmas Tree" and a poignant version of "Hark the Herald Angels Sing," and headed up to their room to spend more time together.

Not that anyone made a late night of it. With three

newborns in the house, and more emotions flying around than was necessary for a family holiday, everyone was ready for an early night.

"You look happy this morning."

Bree rolled over to see Liam propped up on one elbow, staring at her.

"I *am* happy." She reached out and traced the bite mark she'd left on his shoulder.

She'd done that. She'd marked her mate and taken him forever. He was hers.

And she was his.

And Bree didn't think it was possible to be any happier than she was in that moment.

"Do you think it's crazy?" she asked abruptly.

"Is what crazy?"

"With everything that's happened in such a short time," she began. "And everything that I've learned about my family…do you think it's crazy that I'm so happy?"

The thought had hit her a few times last night as they were gathered around, singing and having a good time. *Did it make her a bad person if she was happy? Should she be grieving for the life she'd lost? The life she thought she'd had but didn't? Should she…*

"Not at all." Liam grabbed her and kissed her thoroughly. "It's one of the things I love so much about you."

"That I'm not sad?"

He laughed. "Yes. But more than that," he continued. "I love that you just live life to its fullest. You don't dwell on the past, on things you can't change. You just…live. I think more people should be that way."

She smiled and kissed him on the nose. "Right now I'm just super happy that I get to live with you."

Liam took her hand and rolled to the other side of the bed, pulling her on top of him. "I think we should live a little right now," he teased.

As much as Bree would like nothing more, the voices from downstairs were drifting up the stairs already and that meant one thing. Christmas Day had officially begun and they needed to get down there.

THEY WOULD HAVE their whole life to spend lazy mornings in bed. Liam knew that rationally. Still, he couldn't help but look longingly across the room at his mate.

His mate.

Of course, he would have to be the first to admit that as much as he would have been happy spending the day with his woman in his arms, he was enjoying every minute of Christmas Day with his family. A family that less than a month ago he'd almost lost because of his own pigheadedness.

Thank God things had changed. Thank God *he* had changed.

"You look deep in thought, brother." Natalia pulled up a chair next to him at the table where he'd been sitting. "But you also look very happy."

He turned and gave her a smile. "I am both of those things." He reached over and pulled her in for a quick hug. "Life is damn good, Nat."

Her smile was wide. "It really is, Liam. I honestly never thought we'd be here."

"At Grizzly Ridge?" he teased.

"You know exactly what I mean." She waved her arms to encompass the whole of the room: all of their cousins, and siblings, and mates, and now, their mothers too. Tonia had spent the last day getting to know her children all over again, as well as their mates and the babies. For many people it would be overwhelming, but Tonia seemed to handle it with ease. Particularly after the delivery of baby Noel. A special moment for everyone. "I'm really glad you decided to stay for Christmas," she said. "It was important for you to know how much we all love you, despite…well, despite everything and maybe because of it."

He laughed. "Because of it? I doubt that."

Natalia joined in his laughter. "Okay, I know it sounds crazy. But that's the thing about this family, right? We love and accept each other both despite and because of our craziness."

He looked around the room again. "That's the truth."

"You just needed to forgive yourself, Liam," she added, her voice dipped down a notch. "And I'm really glad you did."

Liam nodded. "Nat? I just wanted to tell you again how—"

"No." She stopped him. "No more apologies, Liam. I told you, we forgave you a long time ago. It's over. The past is the past. I think that Tonia has shown us that. And if her children can forgive everything that's happened, and Bree…" She shook her head in wonder. "With everything Bree has been through, and to have such a good attitude about it all…she really is something else."

Liam couldn't disagree with that. "And she's mine."

Natalia laughed and punched him good-naturedly on the shoulder. "I'm so glad you found someone to put up with you. Now, come on. I don't know about you, but I think it's time for a little Christmas cheer."

THE DAY PASSED in a blur and by the time the family had exchanged a few presents, feasted on the meal of roast turkey with all the fixings, and settled back into the living room, with a roaring fire in the hearth and full bellies, Bree was exhausted. She snuggled into Liam on the couch and from across the room met Tonia's eyes. The older woman looked concerned, but when Bree smiled, she returned it with warmth.

It was still a lot to take in that Tonia was her *aunt*. And despite the way everything had come to be, and the way she'd learned about it all, it felt good to know she had a family—a clan—out there who cared about her. Bree had so many questions for Tonia, so many things she wanted to know and learn. About her parents, her clan…all of it. And she would ask all of those things. But there'd be time for that later. For now, all Bree needed to know was that she was safe. Safe and loved. There were still a few things that would take awhile to process and get over, but she really would be fine.

More than fine. Now that she had Liam, she finally felt as if she was home. And the Jacksons had always felt like family to her. Now they were. Yes, it really was the very best Christmas present.

Even better than the matching stockings Bree had made herself and Liam to go with the rest of the stockings Bree had made for the family before she'd even met Liam. Now they really were all a full family.

Kira, with a baby in her arms, approached Bree. "Would you hold her for a moment, please?" Nash was behind her, and he offered up the other baby to Liam, who took him.

They exchanged a glance. *What was going on?*

After the infants were settled, Kira and Nash turned to face the room. "I think we have something we should tell you all," Kira said.

"You're making it sound so serious." Nash took her hand. "But it is something we should probably let you in on."

"You're not moving back to Yellowstone!"

It was Chloe who called out, but Kade, with his arm around Ella, who was holding their own newborn son, chimed in as well. "No way," he said. "These babies all need to grow up together. And there's no way I'm letting my niece and nephew be raised by—"

"We're not moving." Kira cut him off before he could say

anything about Nash's heritage. The last thing any of them needed was a fight between brothers-in-law. "It's nothing like that at all. We just thought maybe we should tell you that we settled on names finally."

There were a few hoots of laughter from around the room, but Bree couldn't tear her eyes off the perfect little girl in her arms. Her tiny nose, her dark eyelashes that rested on her creamy white cheeks, and her pink lips that were currently pressed together. She was absolutely gorgeous.

"So?" Natalia asked. "We're dying here. What are their names?"

"Holly and Jack," Kira said. "I actually wanted to name her Tonia." She turned and smiled at her mother. "I mean, I didn't know if I was ever going to see you again, and...well, it seemed right." Tonia looked as if she were going to burst into tears. "But then you...well, you're here now. And I'm glad you are, but it didn't feel right then to have two Tonias. I hope that's okay?" There were a few murmurs of agreement. "And because it's Christmas, and...well, I love the name Holly."

"It's a beautiful name."

Bree looked down again at little Holly. "It's perfect."

"And Jack?" It was Liam who asked. "Where did that come from?"

"That's an easy one." Nash spoke up. "We wanted him to have a connection, in name as well as in his heart, with the Jackson clan."

"What do you mean by that?" Axel crossed his arms over his broad chest. "He'll always be connected to the Jackson clan. He's a Jackson."

"He is," Nash said. "But he's also a North. And he's part of the North clan."

The room was silent as everyone took that in. But it made sense. Of course he was part of Nash's clan as well. More so because Nash was a wolf and they didn't know how that was going to work out for the babies. No one would know until they hit puberty and shifted for the first time.

"I like it." Axel nodded. "I like it a lot. They're great names. Holly and Jack North, part of the Jackson clan."

"Always." Kira hugged her big brother. "We'll always be part of the Jackson clan."

"Enough with all the hugs and crying. It's Christmas!" Cyrus and Ryker stood and went to the bar in the corner, where they refreshed everyone's drinks. "And now for the really important stuff," Ryker said as he handed Harper a glass of wine. "Who won the Reindeer Games?" He gave her a wink and a subtle little nudge with his elbow.

"Yeah. Who won?" someone else called out.

Harper took a sip of wine and laughed as everyone grew serious again, all eyes on her while they waited in anticipation for the announcement.

But Harper only laughed and shrugged. "We all won."

"What?"

"No way!"

"We won."

"We were definitely the fastest at the race!"

"Did you hear us crank out '*Rudolph*' last night? We're the winners."

Everyone spoke at once and Harper held up her hands with a laugh. "I know, I know. And I really did intend on picking winners, but...well, things got kind of crazy around here. I mean, you guys all had babies!"

Ella laughed. "It's okay, *mi amiga*. There's always next year. Then we can all play."

"You never know." Liam looked at Bree. "A lot can change in a year. Maybe we'll have a cub of our own?"

Bree blushed, but the idea hit her right in the heart. She looked down at the sleeping infant still in her arms and then back to Liam.

A lot of things *could* change in a year.

She gave him the slightest nod and blew him a kiss. "You are living proof of that, my love."

I hope you've enjoyed the Bears of Grizzly Ridge as much as I've enjoyed writing them.
In fact, I've had SO much fun writing my sexy bears that I'll definitely be revisiting shifters again in the future.
Until then, you may not know that I also write contemporary romance. If you're in the mood for something a little different, please check out an excerpt of Love in the Moment right after this. **One click Love in the Moment for FREE right now!**

AND…don't forget to join my mailing list where you'll be the first to hear about new stories, sales and promotions and giveaways!
You can join me here —>
https://elenaaitken.com/newsletter/

Love in the Moment

Please enjoy this excerpt from Love in the Moment.

IAN MCCORMICK STOLE a glance at the woman sitting next to him. He'd picked her up only ten minutes earlier from the bus station and already he'd run out of things to talk about. In fact, beyond the general introductions they'd exchanged, they really hadn't spoken at all. He felt as if he should say something to break the silence, but every time he opened his mouth, he drew a blank. What was he supposed to say to the younger half-sister he'd never met?

The sister that he'd never had any desire to meet, not since finding out about her existence almost ten years ago. As far as he was concerned, Ian could have gone the rest of his life without knowing about Chelsea or her sister, Amber's existence. And he really didn't see any need to get to know either of them. After all, they were the reason his entire life had imploded all those years ago.

Okay, that wasn't entirely fair. It wasn't their fault that their father had led a secret life, with a completely different family. A family he'd finally left his *other* family for, leaving Ian, his brothers, and his mother all alone. *No. It wasn't the girls' fault.* But all of the reasoning in the world hadn't made it any easier for Ian to wrap his head around it. Despite the fact that it had been almost a decade ago.

He snuck another look at the girl who had barely looked up from her phone since she'd sat down in the jeep. There was definitely a family resemblance. She had their father's green eyes, just like he did. And the dark, thick hair. He hated to admit it, but there was no denying she was his sister. And it wasn't as if he could spend the whole summer not talking to her. He'd made a promise to Declan, his second youngest brother.

"It's not her fault," Declan had said on the phone. *"Chelsea and Amber aren't to blame, Ian. You need to get over it."*

Dec was right. He did need to get over it, especially since she was going to be staying with him all summer. He took a breath and opened his mouth to say something, but didn't have a chance.

"I know you hate me."

Ian shut his mouth dumbly.

"And I suppose you think you have a reason to," Chelsea continued. "But it wasn't my idea to come here, you know? Declan pretty much insisted that it would be *good for me* or something, and…well…I kinda trust Dec. Besides, I didn't really have anywhere else to go."

He swallowed hard, giving himself a moment. "I don't hate you." As he spoke the words, he realized they were true. "I just don't know you. And Declan's right. It will be good for you here."

"You don't even know why he said that."

"I don't need to." Ian slowed the jeep to take the turn that would lead them out of town, toward the cottages. His house sat at the end of a row of other log cabins that were used primarily by summer people. Most of the houses were built by families who came from the city for the summer months, and they were still locked up tight because the season wouldn't start for another month or so. It was quiet, but Ian liked it. At least for now, while he was getting settled. And it was true, he didn't know why Declan thought it was a good idea for Chelsea to get out of the city for the summer, but he had a few guesses, and there was no doubt that a little bit of quiet would be good for her, too. "I trust Declan, too," he said as the jeep bumped over the dirt road. It was impossible not to trust Declan. Out of all of his siblings, Dec was definitely the most trustworthy, and the most compassionate and caring and…he was pretty much everything good in the world. "If he thinks it'll be good for you out here, he's probably right."

She shrugged and turned back to her cell phone, looking up a moment later in horror. "The service is terrible here."

"One of my favorite features." He smiled.

"Why would that be a good thing?"

He ignored the question. "It's not that bad, really. Just a little spotty sometimes. Besides, you'll be able to get Wi-Fi at the Dockside as soon as I get it hooked up."

"The Dockside?"

"The new marina." Ian couldn't help but smile. "Cool name, right?" The main reason he'd returned to Cedar Springs was because the economy was starting to pick up, and there were business opportunities to be had. One of the first he'd found was the old marina. It was just next to the Grizzly Paw on the beach in town and Ian remembered it as *the* meeting place for summer fun. He picked it up for a bargain basement price, probably because it needed so much work. By the looks of things, it had sat empty for years and it would definitely take a little elbow grease to get it up and running again. Not that Ian was afraid of hard work. In fact, that had always been his favorite part of a new business: turning nothing into something. "I just closed on it yesterday. And with any luck, it will be open and ready for business in time for the season to start. But if that's going to happen, I'm going to need a little help."

She looked at him sideways. "And I suppose you want me to help."

"You got it. Call it...the price of admission."

She rolled her eyes and shoved her phone into her duffel bag. "Why not? I guess a summer job won't hurt."

"Oh no." Ian braced himself for her response to what he was about to tell her. "Helping at the marina isn't a summer job—it's just an expectation. I got you a job, too. You'll be starting at the Grizzly Paw right away. Sam's an old friend of mine, and she's doing me a favor by giving you this job, so I know you won't let me down."

"Two jobs?"

"No." He shook his head. "Just one. And a family project."

"But I'm never going to have any time to have fun," she wailed.

That was the point, at least as far as Ian was concerned. He didn't know much about twenty-two-year-old girls, but from what Declan had told him, Chelsea was making far too many poor choices. And as the big brother—whether he wanted to be or not—it was going to be his job to help her make good ones. Or keep her too busy to make anything but.

WHEN GWEN HENDERSON had dreamed of her triumphant return to Cedar Springs after years of hard work and sacrifice, she'd dreamed of driving an expensive convertible down Main Street, her dark hair floating in the breeze as all the men's heads turned to see the beautiful and famous celebrity she'd turned out to be as they kicked themselves for not dating her when they had their chance.

Yes, in her fantasies, it was perfect. In reality, however, she had not imagined that on the eve of her summer visit to Cedar Springs, her secondhand Mustang would have some random, and likely expensive, engine problem that would require her taking the bus into town. And she most certainly did not expect that the one man who'd not only turned her down as a teenager, but had publicly humiliated her ten years earlier at the Summer Equinox Festival, would be there when she got off the bus.

Ian McCormick.

He didn't even *live* in Cedar Springs. What were the odds the one man who still haunted—no, not haunted...*visited*—her dreams would not only be standing there when she got off the stupid, humiliating bus, but would also look her square in the eye and not even recognize her?

If she was honest with herself, and she'd made that a habit over the last few years, that was the part that hurt the most. Ian McCormick had been her biggest teenage crush. No, her *only* teenage crush. Every summer for four years, she had lusted after him. Practically threw herself at him that final summer. But he'd barely even noticed her and when she thought she'd finally had a date with him at the festival, he'd stood her up. Left her there all alone. She knew now he'd only said yes to the date out of pity. After all, it didn't make sense for someone as handsome and smart as Ian McCormick to go out with fat, pimple-faced, four-eyed, frizzy-haired *Giant Gigi*. At the time, she'd been heartbroken—totally destroyed, really. But time and distance had taught her social order. The other thing time and distance had taught her was the impact that health, fitness, contacts, clear skin, a new hair-do, and a name change could do for social order.

It had been five years since she'd dropped the stupid childhood nickname, adopted a fitness regime and lost seventy-five pounds, finding herself and a new career in the process. Early on in her transformation, Gwen decided to document everything on social media, using a blog and then a Facebook and Instagram account to chronicle her progress. The result was not only a whole new body, but also a very loyal following, commercial and marketing deals, and the potential for a book and maybe even a reality television show. She was a very different person than the sad, overweight teenager she'd been on her summer visits to see her grandma in Cedar Springs. *Very* different. And with women looking up to her and men lining up to date her, she no longer needed Ian McCormick to validate her worth.

But if that was true, why had her heart done a stupid little flip when he'd grabbed her bag at the bus stop? And why had her pulse raced out of control when he looked at her? How was it even possible that he could still have that effect on her after all these years?

"Gwen!"

Deanna Gordon shot out of the building across the street and without even looking, raced across the street and pulled her into a hug. "Oh my goodness, you look amazing." Deanna held her out at arm's length for a fraction of a second before she pulled her back into a hug. "I'm so glad you're finally here. I was going to meet you at the bus stop—that's crazy that your car broke down—but I got caught up with a patient and—"

"It's okay." Gwen finally cut her off with a laugh. "I literally only walked half a block. Don't worry about it."

Deanna bent down and scooped up her bag. "Is this all you have? One duffel bag? I don't think I could travel that light if I tried."

Gwen laughed again. "Are you kidding? The rest of my bags are coming later. I may have sweet-talked the guy at the depot to deliver them personally."

"You did not?"

She only smiled in response. It wasn't often that Gwen used her curves and killer smile to get her way, but sometimes she couldn't seem to help herself. Besides, it's not as though she did it very often.

Deanna shook her head, but her friend smiled. "Hey, if you can get away with it…why not, right?"

"Exactly. And heaven knows I haven't always had this skill. I might as well take advantage sometimes. But don't tell anyone, okay?"

Deanna stared at her. "Who would I tell?"

She forgot sometimes that not everyone lived their whole life online. For Gwen, it was normal to record everything, and censor anything she didn't want getting out. It was a carefully constructed existence, one that was almost entirely public, because she'd built her following by *not* keeping very much private. Her readers liked to hear everything about her, including her workouts, what she had for dinner, her dates, and even more personal things about her dating habits. Not that she'd had much to report lately. She may get a lot of attention from men, but that attention disappeared pretty quickly when they found out who she was and what she did for a living.

"Forget it." Gwen shrugged it off. "I didn't really mean it like that. I mean…"

"I keep forgetting what you do for a living," Deanna said. "I mean, it's crazy to me that you can do that for a *job*. Oh, but I didn't mean it like that. I'm sorry, Gwen. It's just—"

"It's fine. I totally get it. It is crazy. I'm not offended." She decided to change tact and confide in the one person who would totally understand. "But you know what *did* offend me?"

Her friend froze on the sidewalk and waited.

"Ian McCormick." She pronounced every syllable of his name with an edge.

"Ian? You saw him?"

"You know he's here?"

Deanna blinked at her mildly before she put a smile back on her face and ushered Gwen down the sidewalk. "You know what? Let's drop your bag off and then you can tell me all about it over a cup of coffee."

Gwen eyed her friend and shook her head. "How about a *drink*?"

"WHY DIDN'T you tell me Ian McCormick was here?" Gwen sat across from Deanna at her kitchen table, a glass of soda water in her hand. She'd gone for the soda, deciding against alcohol. It was her default drink, but now that she had it, she wished she'd gone for something stronger after all. *Ian McCormick was in Cedar Springs.* That had not been part of the plan. Not at all. Sure, whenever she thought of her summers in Cedar Springs visiting her grandma, Ian figured largely in her memory. Whether he knew it or not, his attention—or lack thereof, as was the case—had figured largely in her teenage life. She couldn't remember a summer she hadn't spent lusting after him. As one of the *summer* kids, he was kind of a celebrity among the local kids. Not that she'd been a local kid. But she also wasn't a summer kid. Gwen had definitely floated and never really had any friends except for Deanna.

Ian had no shortage of girls after him, but he'd never wanted to date any of them.

No. That wasn't true. He just hadn't wanted to date *her*. Not that she could blame him. If she'd been a teenage boy back then, *she* wouldn't have wanted to date her. Almost a hundred pounds overweight, with bad hair and glasses, she was a walking cliché. Hell, she was even more of a cliché now that she'd lost all the weight, turned her life around and was returning to her past childhood haunts. She was a made-for-TV movie, for goodness sake.

"I honestly didn't think it mattered." Deanna joined her at the table. "He's a summer kid."

"A...he's not a kid anymore. And, B...you know he's way more than that. He's *way more.*"

Deanna almost spat out her water. "No."

"No what?"

"No way you still have a thing for Ian McCormick."

Gwen didn't even have to answer that question, because the woman she'd always considered to be her best friend knew her well enough to know the answer. Or, she should have known her better than that, anyway. She narrowed her eyes and tilted her head.

"No way." Deanna shook her head. "Gwen, how can you possibly still be hung up on him? Honestly, I thought maybe after...well..."

"We said we'd never talk about that, remember?"

The situation they were never to discuss was a moment that could have broken up their friendship forever, but the girls made a decision not to let it affect them. Even though it had been hard, very hard for Gwen. The last summer she'd come to visit, Ian had arrived earlier than he usually had and somehow, Deanna and Ian ended up together at a party where they drank too much and...Gwen didn't like to think about it, but Deanna lost her virginity to Ian McCormick. She could have let it destroy their friendship, but Deanna felt terribly about it and she swore she'd never been more than just a friend with Ian and that's all it would ever be.

"Still," Deanna said. "I honestly didn't think you'd still be thinking of him at all."

How could she not? When they were kids, he'd actually been nice to her. He even talked to her and the conversations they had were real. Not about stupid stuff where she had to pretend to be interested in whatever football team was going to the playoffs or who got drunk at whatever party. But real stuff like what they hoped to achieve with their lives, what the future looked like and where they wanted to go to college. And besides that, he'd been so gorgeous. Correction, he *was* gorgeous. Maybe even more so, if that was possible.

But he still doesn't know you're alive, Gwen, the little voice in her head reminded her. She wasn't more than a townie friend back then, and she was even less now.

"So, he didn't recognize you?" Deanna changed tack. "Not that I'm surprised. You look like a totally different person. Seriously, if I didn't know better, I wouldn't even recognize you and we've been friends since…well, forever. You look crazy good."

Gwen blushed and waved away the compliment. She couldn't seem to get used to the attention she got from people who knew her *when.* It was almost easier for people to think she was just naturally thin and fit. Except when it came to her blog. But talking about her experiences online was a totally different thing. It was safe to hide behind the screen.

In fact, throughout her transformation, it had been a sort of therapy almost. Her website was the place she went to decompress and work through all the feelings that went along with her journey.

She should blog about Ian. Why hadn't she thought of that earlier? It made perfect sense. She could have a chance to process her feelings about seeing him again. *And still being invisible.* And she'd already made her summer vacation into an *event.* When she'd announced her plans to return to Cedar Springs, her readers had gone wild. They wrote in, offering suggestions as to how she should present her transformed self to her old friends, what she should do for a part-time job, and pretty much everything in between. It never ceased to amaze her how invested her readers were in her life and her weight loss journey. In fact, the whole *returning home* thing had garnered so much attention that a talent agent, Jade Johnson, had contacted Gwen about representation, a book deal, and a possible television deal. It was all too crazy to comprehend, but Gwen wasn't about to say no.

She swallowed the rest of her water quickly. "The next one needs alcohol."

"Really?"

Gwen nodded. "Yes. There are only sixty-four calories in vodka. And I'll just run a few extra miles tomorrow. It'll be worth it."

Deanna laughed. "Sounds good. Well, not the running part. I'll leave that up to you. But I don't have any patients tomorrow, so I'll have a few drinks to toast your return. I'll get Marcus to meet us at the Grizzly Paw when he's done up at the hill. He'll want to meet you. I have trouble remembering that you never knew him."

"Nope." Gwen shook her head. "He moved here after my last summer. But it sounds like a good plan to me." Gwen leaned down to retrieve her laptop from the bag at her feet. "But first I need to post an entry."

"Seriously? You just got here."

"I know." She smiled and tried not to take offense to her friend's expression. Ever since her blog started to get real attention and had actually started to make her money, most people had the same reaction. She'd definitely discovered that people struggled with the idea that you could actually make a living writing about your life. Hell, when the advertising offers had first started coming in, Gwen had trouble believing anyone would actually want to give her money to tell her story. "But it pays the bills, Dee. So as long as people want to read it, I'm going to write it."

She flipped open her laptop, signed onto Deanna's Wi-Fi and logged into her account before her fingers froze over the keys. "What do you think?" she asked her friend. "How should I write about Ian?"

"Ian?" Deanna shook her head. "You can't. I mean, you can't use his name or anything."

"Oh my God. Of course not! I don't use anyone's real name. I don't even say what town I'm in. That part is all anonymous. It has to be. But part of the success of everything is how real it all is. So…"

"You're going to blog about Ian?"

Gwen nodded. There really wasn't a question about it. In fact, she'd already kind of alluded to him in past posts as one of her catalysts for starting her weight loss journey. There was no doubt in her mind that if she'd been thin all those years ago, Ian would never have stood her up at the Summer Equinox festival. Not a chance.

"Wait." Deanna got that look in her eye that meant she'd just figured out the connection. "You've already blogged about him, haven't you?"

"You read my blog?"

Deanna gave her a look. "Of course I do. Since the beginning. And that's when you mentioned…Ian is Mr. Summer. How did I not see that until right now?"

Gwen laughed. "I have no idea. It's not like my feelings for him were a big secret or anything. Doesn't everyone remember my public humiliation?"

Deanna grabbed her hand and squeezed. "Gwen, no one remembers that. I promise."

"I remember."

Her friend laughed a little and moved away. "You're the only one. It wasn't even a big deal. He just didn't show up. It's not important. Let it go."

But as Deanna moved about the kitchen, cleaning up dishes and leaving Gwen to write her blog post, all she could think of was that it *was* important and there was no way she could let it go.

DEAR READER,

SOMETIMES THINGS DON'T TURN out quite the way you plan...

IF YOU'RE anything like me, you've spent some time thinking about and maybe even daydreaming about how certain people from your past will react to seeing the new and healthier version of you after wronging you. Not to say that I've spent a lot of time thinking on this, but I'd be lying if I said I never thought of it. Of course, as I was planning my return to the town I'd spent all my summers, there was one person in particular that came to mind. Mr. Summer. Long-time readers will remember me mentioning Mr. Summer before. Every young woman—particularly those of us who've struggled with our body image...who hasn't—has at least one encounter with a boy or man that has stuck with them. An encounter for better or worse that somehow shaped or defined how they thought of members of the opposite sex, and sadly, how they thought of themselves.

That was Mr. Summer. I was desperately in love with him from the summers of fourteen to eighteen. Four years of my life in which he barely knew I was alive. When he finally did notice me, he humiliated me and broke my heart.

For years, he was the star of my fantasies when I thought about returning with my new and improved self. How would he react? Would his jaw drop? Would he stumble over his words as he apologized for standing me up all those years ago? Would he beg me to give him another chance?

WELL, readers, I can tell you that now, all these years later I finally have my answer.

None of those things happened. In fact, he didn't even recognize me.

We came eye to eye and there wasn't even a flicker of acknowledgment in his eyes. (Which are still as dreamy as I remember.)

And now I'm here, on the eve of my first night back in town and already I'm filled with a strong sense of dissatisfaction in regards to Mr. Summer. So, obviously I cannot let a homecoming come and go without doing something about it. Or can I?

WHAT DO YOU THINK? *Should I confront Mr. Summer and thank him for being at least one of the catalysts that spurred my life change? Or should I let it go and move on? Or maybe something different….*

Read the rest of **Love in the Moment** NOW!

About the Author

Elena Aitken is a USA Today Bestselling Author of more than forty romance and women's fiction novels. Living a stone's throw from the Rocky Mountains with her teenager twins, their two cats and a goofy rescue dog, Elena escapes into the mountains whenever life allows. She can often be found with her toes in the lake and a glass of wine in her hand, dreaming up her next book and working on her own happily ever after with her very own mountain man.

To learn more about Elena:
www.elenaaitken.com
elena@elenaaitken.com

www.ingramcontent.com/pod-product-compliance
Lightning Source LLC
Chambersburg PA
CBHW050841180626
46814CB00007B/2569